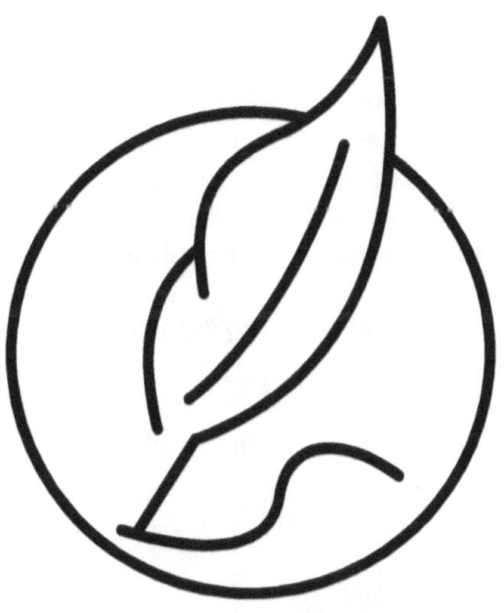

a spilt ink press novel

Published by Spilt Ink Press. First edition, 2026.

Spilt Ink Press is an imprint of Gordon Publishing Collective dedicated to transformative storytelling born from life's beautiful messes. We believe the stains of experience hold magic—and from every spill, a story can rise.

www.spiltink.press
www.gordonpublishingco.com
info@gordonpublishingco.com

ISBN: 978-1-970895-01-8

Take Care

of Our

Daughter

By Emily Mulcahey

For my brother, Dan.
Thank you for being my first reader and second-worst critic.

PROLOGUE

FALL 2095

*I*F YOU'RE READING THIS, IT MEANS THE HUMAN RACE SURVIVED.

I should start by saying that I'm somebody to you, but to everyone else, I'm nobody. No one will build statues in my name, or remember me at all, for that matter. But I had a great life, I want that to be clear. Like most people, a lot of it was spent just trying to survive, but I still feel lucky to have had it. In the end, it brought me—and more importantly, you—to where we both are now.

To be honest, I got a lot more time than most people did. A lot more time than I probably deserved. Most of the people I love did, too. And in the end, that's what matters.

Right now, in the quiet, I wanted to get some words down. I hope more than anything that one day, you'll read them. I need you and everyone else to understand what happened— why we did what we did. To understand that the people who were left weren't all bad. To understand that, when it came to the end, we never gave up.

History has a way of being manipulated. I guess I don't have much control over that, but I wanted to give you the truth. Do with it what you will.

WINTER 2053

Then

It was the Saturday morning before Christmas, ninety degrees and sunny in Fort Collins, Colorado.

The sound of laughing children echoed through the streets downtown, where most of the sixth-grade class had gathered for a pick-up baseball game. Some of their grandparents peered down through the windows of nearby homes to watch. They could all remember seeing snow this time of year in their childhood, but their grandkids never would.

By 2053, a lot of the elderly folks couldn't go outside at all. They couldn't take the heat. Literally. The change had started slowly. Oil company by oil company, degree by degree, and these grandparents had been there for it all. They spent most days indoors, wondering what would come next. But watching this young generation play outside gave them hope for whatever that may be.

Out on the field below, Bobby stepped up to the plate. Four feet, eight inches of knobby knees, red hair, and freckles.

"Aye battah battah!" his best friend Rory shouted from where she stood on second base. "Send me home!"

Bobby smiled. Cool, calm, and collected as always when he got up to bat. He got picked on in school constantly, but not here. On the baseball diamond, he was king. He could hit the ball further than every kid on this field, and they all knew it. He loosened his grip, breathed out slowly, and looked the pitcher—Vince—in the eyes, waiting.

Vince was Public Enemy Number One for Bobby and Rory. His bullying was as vicious as it was relentless. They'd all been friends in lower elementary school, but in the third grade, Bobby made the mistake of confiding in Vince that he'd wet his bed the night before. A terrifying prospect for a nine-year-old. Vince had seized his moment at potential popularity and immediately coined the nickname that had followed Bobby for the last three years: "bed wetter." Original.

But here, now, on the field, they both knew the score: Bobby was the better ball player, bed wetting notwithstanding.

Vince smirked—his only defense—and threw.

The pitch came in, lobbing toward Bobby in a perfect arc. He thought it was the most beautiful thing he'd ever seen. His eyes betrayed a flash of eagerness. His right Nike dug into the earth firmly. His hands came forward first, bringing around the bat with an audible *whoosh.* As soon as metal connected with cowhide, he felt it. It was gone, *sayonara,* and each and every little head on the field watched it go. It soared over the outfield, over the fence, and landed across the street.

At first, Rory jumped up and down on second base, cheering and whooping for an obvious home run. Then she stopped. Both teams stopped. The ball hit the ground on the other side of the street and rolled. With bated breath, they all watched as it continued on into the darkness, where they could not follow.

"*Great,*" said Vince. "Game's over. Nice job, bed wetter."

Bobby felt an immediate rush of heat swell from his neck all the way to his forehead.

"N—nobody's got another ball?" he asked.

"No, dumbass," piped up another voice—Alex, Vince's second in command. "Can't you stick to ruining your bed instead of our games?"

"Shove it, Alex," Rory said. "You're just jealous because you suck. Way to go, Bob, we won!"

Vince turned on Rory, flashing that smirk again. Rory was another target for Vince and his cronies because she was a girl and she was better than all of them on the field, too. "Why don't you tell your little boyfriend to go get it?" he said.

Rory rolled her eyes. One strand of brown hair hung out of her baseball cap and one hand rested on her hip. "Hilarious. Why don't *you* go get it if you're so brave?"

"Because I didn't hit it over there!"

"Yeah well maybe if you weren't such a shitty pitcher—!"

"It's fine, Rory," Bobby interjected. He swallowed hard. "I'll get it."

Silence. Every pair of eyes had turned to him.

"What the hell are you talking about?" Rory said. "We're just messing around. No one's getting it."

But Bobby knew. This was it. This was the moment that would define him. It could change everything for him at school. Nobody went into the dark. *Nobody.* But if *he* did…

He threw his bat to the ground. "I'm going," he said, and started across the field.

Rory stepped directly into his path as he approached. "Bobby!" she said, breathing hard. "Bobby. Stop! Are you crazy? Just leave it. Who cares? It's a ball!"

He brushed by her, picking up his pace.

"It's just a *ball,*" Rory said again, chasing after him. "Let's just go back to my place and eat lunch."

Bobby ignored her, trudging on. He went through the

outfield and climbed over the fence, a mob of twenty kids in his wake. He could hear the fence rattling behind him as one by one, they all followed.

"Stop, Bobby!" Rory yelled, her footsteps clacking across the narrow street as she finally caught up to him.

But he couldn't. He'd committed now.

They reached the edge of the sunlight. It would be a few years before the wall went up in an effort to keep people from doing exactly what Bobby was about to do. But most people wouldn't need a wall to keep them from stepping over the line. The grandparents, who'd mostly gone back to their sitcoms now, remembered a time when kids were taught not to take rides from strangers. But these days, that was the stuff of legends. The people who remained in the light today taught their children only one rule: never go into the dark.

Bobby stood looking into the inky black. He was less than a foot away but still, no matter how much he strained his eyes, he saw nothing. The darkness cut across the earth in a straight line. On the side where they stood now, the earth lived in perpetual sunlight. One step away, everything else— *whatever* else—lived in perpetual darkness.

It must be right there, Bobby thought. *I'll only be in there for a second.*

People had gone in and come out before, he knew. But more often than not, they were never seen again. The crowd gathered behind Bobby, who was now only inches from the edge.

"Bobby, please," Rory said from over his left shoulder. "Don't."

Behind him, Bobby heard his classmates murmur and shift. If he'd turned back, he'd have seen that even Vince had gone white. *Would he really do it?*

Bobby stepped forward. Rory risked another step closer and put a firm hand on his shoulder, holding him back. "Don't," she said again.

Bobby turned to her. "It'll be one second! It's right there. I know it. I can do this." He dropped his voice. "I can't turn back now," he whispered, gesturing to the huge crowd of kids behind her—all of them staring at him in awe. "Think about how cool this will make us when we get back to school!" His eyes were pleading, huge with the hope of turning "bed wetter" into "darkness conqueror."

"I'll be right back," he said.

Rory turned to look at the crowd of kids gathered behind them. For that fraction of a second, her attention wavered. Bobby shook his arm free and crossed the line.

Rory felt his shirt slip out of her hand. She snapped her head back around to where he'd just been standing, but he was gone. Completely consumed by the darkness beyond. Behind her, she heard the crowd gasp. For one moment, she thought about how she and Bobby would tell this story at lunch after the Christmas break.

Then she heard it.

The sound of something shuffling on the other side—something moving toward them—a *chittering* noise. It was fast. And somehow, Rory knew it was *hungry*. She heard Bobby start to scream, but the sound was sliced out of the air before it even left her friend's throat. The children jumped.

"BOBBY!" Rory yelled. "BOBBY! COME BACK!" She took one shaking step forward, her toe touching the black line across the earth, and strained her eyes as she searched through the blackness in front of her.

She could hear it on the other side—it's wet breathing, in

and out. She could *feel* something looking back—straining further and further to reach her. If she held out a hand, she knew she could touch it. But she saw nothing.

For a moment, that was it. Just the sound of that heavy, ragged breath against the backdrop of complete silence from the kids behind her. They stood in a pack, mouths agape, frozen in terror.

Then a baseball rolled toward them out of the darkness.

It was followed by a trail of dark, red blood.

2076

Now

Rory

Rory's eyes snap open. She lays statue still and listens.

Crunch.

Something is just outside their tent, walking over the ocean of dead leaves. It's getting closer.

The all-too-familiar sensation of her heart lurching into her throat pushes her into action. Silently, she rolls over to face her sleeping daughter and slips a hand out of her sleeping bag, covering Sarah's mouth. The girl's eyes open—Rory doesn't miss the flash of terror in them—but Sarah remains quiet, listening.

Crunch. Crunch.

Rory looks at her daughter but doesn't need to tell her: *be quiet.*

Crunch crunch crunch.

It's right on top of them now. The moon has been huge the last few days, so Rory can just make out its silhouette against the tent.

Crunch.

She sighs with relief. A deer.

Rory removes her hand from Sarah's mouth. "Sorry," she says, rubbing tiredly at the scar on her face.

"It's okay, Mom," Sarah answers.

Rory looks at her daughter and the guilt sets in, as it always does. What an awful world for a person to grow up in. Sarah will never have a real childhood. She'll never play sports. Never go to prom. Never fall in love.

All of her memories will be made in darkness. This makes her think of Bobby— her poor friend all those years ago—and shudder.

The darkness finally consumed everything about two years ago. Two years of no sunlight. No flowers, no warmth, no normalcy.

And four years with no Matt.

Each time she looks at Sarah now, she's still struck by how much she looks like her father. At fifteen, Sarah has long blonde hair that she always keeps in a braid over her shoulder. Her green eyes are, to Rory, the only bright thing in this dark world. Sarah is tall with lean, muscled arms from two years of building and dismantling camp.

They pack up the tent in a matter of minutes.

"You want to lead today?" Rory asks.

"Sure," Sarah says, taking the map and compass.

They set off north. Always north.

. . .

They break for camp around 6 p.m. every day. In a world that's always dark, there's no such thing as a circadian rhythm. They could've simply adapted to sleeping when they were tired and moving when they weren't, but Rory wanted to keep some semblance of routine if only for her own sanity. She'd found a battery-operated watch in one of the dozens of decrepit, cleared-out towns they'd passed through over the years and started using it to schedule their days. Rise at 6 a.m., camp at 6 p.m. Stay alive in the hours between.

Their days are spent walking through the cold, dead remains of the western United States. Sometimes they get lucky and find an abandoned cabin they can use for a few days or weeks if they feel like resting. But mostly, they move like smoke through what's left of the U.S. after The Collapse—silently, and hopefully difficult to track.

"Mom?" Sarah whispers into the blackness of their tent after they curl up for sleep that night.

"Yeah?"

"Tell me about Dad again."

Rory smiles. "What do you want to know?"

"Anything."

Rory sighs. Sarah asks about her dad a lot. "Well," she says, "he was the best. We met when we were really young, and we sort of grew up together. He had blond hair like yours. You look like him more every day."

"Tell me about the light."

Rory cringes. She doesn't think she'll ever get used to that. "You remember the light, Sarah."

"I know, but I like the way you talk about it."

Rory remembers sitting on a blanket in the sun with Matt. They used to head up to the high school football field to drink cheap beer and daydream about the future. Back when they had no idea what was coming—no idea that the darkness was expanding with speed, or that they'd live to see the deterioration of mankind, or that they only had a few short years left together. No, back then their biggest worries were about math tests and contraception. She could still feel the warmth of the sun on her face, the way it made his green eyes shine so brightly.

"It used to be warm," Rory says. "Really warm. We didn't even have clothes like this," she said, gesturing at their heavy winter gear. When the darkness had started to expand, winter clothing made a fierce comeback both legally and on the black market. Between that and what she'd been able to find rummaging through her parents' old things, Rory had made out well.

"The sky was blue," she continued. "The sun used to be out all the time, it helped plants grow, helped make people stronger and happier. But sometimes, people got weaker from it because it was always out."

"They did?" Sarah asks.

"They did. Even your grandparents couldn't be outside much when they got older. A lot of scientists weren't sure the earth would even survive that much sunlight."

Sarah snorted. "Wish they could see us now," she said.

Rory laughed. "You could see a lot further when it was light out, too."

"Well, I can see pretty far now," Sarah says.

"Yeah that's true," Rory yawns, running a hand through her buzzed brown hair. She'd sheared it off two years ago, knowing it would be easier—and safer—to travel with short hair.

Because Sarah was still growing the last few years while they'd been in total darkness, her eyes and other senses had adapted to it like an owl.

"You think we're almost there?" Sarah yawns, though she knows how far they still have left to walk.

"Yeah," Rory says. "I think we are."

"You say that every night," Sarah says.

And it's true.

2062

Then

Rory

"Sources have confirmed *that the portion of the earth that resides in sunlight is, in fact, getting smaller.*" Rory heard from the television in the living room. She was only half-listening, as most new parents are at all times. But she felt her heart accelerate at those words. She thought back to that baseball game, all those years ago. About that *thing* she'd heard beyond the curtain of darkness.

The fact was the darkness hadn't been much of an issue as long as they stayed away from it. A few years after her friend Bobby died, the democratic U.S. president had made a landmark decision to divert all funding from the border and, instead, use it to start building a wall across the darkness, effectively abandoning parts of the country that had already been enveloped by the constant night. The bill was also signed by the leaders of Canada and Mexico in a desperate attempt to keep the citizens of North America from wandering off and, of course, to keep whatever was out there, out. The decision triggered protests, outrage, and civil unrest. Ultimately it proved nearly useless. What authorities had tried and failed to keep under wraps was that, wall or no wall, the darkness was closing in. It had already consumed large parts of Europe, Asia, and Russia, in turn ending the U.S. involvement in the wars there, but killing most of their inhabitants.

Criminals over the years had used the darkness as a threat of violence—and as a means of actual violence—by driving people out a few miles and leaving them there to fend for themselves. Sometimes the people left out there came back. Most of the time they didn't.

But in Rory's little life, the darkness hadn't posed much of a threat. And until it did, she had the job of being a mother to do.

She was cooking tonight, navigating the kitchen in the shade of the evening curtains, which cast a soft yellow glow across the room. In an hour or so, she'd put down the blackouts so that Sarah could get some sleep—a habit she'd learned from her own mother as a child.

Tonight, she was cooking a pasta dish. For the sauce, she used vegetables from her garden. Tomatoes and basil did well in the constant sunlight, but she had to replant constantly. Sooner or later, everything began to wither. She'd picked up the pasta at the grocery store downtown, which had switched to solar energy like most businesses years ago. But many businesses in town had been in the direct path of the darkness. Rory had known several small business owners who'd been put out by the dark, losing everything they'd spent their whole lives building.

"What's that, Sarah?" Rory asked her toddler, pointing to the sliced tomato on the counter.

"Mato!" the one-year-old shrieked.

"Yes, that's good! Tomato!"

Sarah responded by slapping her sippy cup and spilling apple juice all over the floor. Rory sighed.

The front door opened and closed, signaling Matt was home from work. He walked into the kitchen and Rory could see that his fluorescent shirt and jeans were covered in paint. They'd known each other since childhood and still, Rory was always struck by how handsome he was. She had no idea how she'd gotten so lucky. When they were just nineteen years old, an unexpected Sarah had come along, but they were happy about it. Their grandparents had grown up in a different world, a world where sunlight didn't rule. Rory's grandmother had worked her way up to becoming a managing editor at a major publishing house, Matt's had been a pharmacist. But when the change began, priorities had shifted. Having people to love and food on the table was more than enough. She and Matt loved each other, and somehow, she loved him even more seeing him become a dad.

Matt looked at Sarah and smiled. "Guess she doesn't love the apple juice, either," he said. "How many is that now? Orange, apple, cranberry..." he grabbed a paper towel to clean up the mess.

"There's a glass of wine for you on the counter," Rory said.

"I *knew* there was a reason I loved you," he said. Wine was difficult to come by since it could only be made in a controlled environment. She'd spent a month on a waitlist for this red.

Matt walked up behind her and wrapped his arms around her waist.

"Hey!" she yelled, pretending to swat him. "You'll get paint all over me!"

He squeezed her. "It's dry, I promise! Besides, if it's *not*, that means I get to clean it off you later..."

Rory had no idea then that she'd look back on this moment years later from the inside of a tent in the middle of the darkness and still feel his body pressed against her. She'd remember how safe she felt with this little family in their little house, making pasta and drinking red wine.

By the time Matt had clinked his glass with hers and started to help with dinner, Rory had completely tuned out the noise from the television in the background.

"As the darkness expands more rapidly, we're going to see a lot of changes."

2076

Now

RORY

EVERY MORNING, Rory spends half a second in bliss. For one, tiny moment, Matt is still here. She can still feel his arms around her when she wakes up. In some masochistic way, she looks forward to sleeping so she can dream of him.

But then she opens her eyes and remembers, and the weight settles back on her chest. An old friend.

She checks her watch and sees that it's just past 6 a.m. And just like it is every day, it's freezing. As they head north, it will only get colder, and she can't shake the fact that she's afraid of just how cold that will be. She knows they're well-prepared—she spent months venturing out into the anarchy to gather supplies before they left. But still, she's never been that far north, and even if she had, the darkness has changed everything.

Over the last few days, the moonlight has begun to wane. First a halfmoon, then smaller and smaller each day. Soon, there will be no moon—the worst two days of the month, when they're plunged into complete and utter darkness. Total darkness means the crits are at their worst.

Sarah yawns, rolls over, and opens her eyes.

"Morning," Rory says

"Morning," Sarah says groggily. She pulls her sleeping bag tighter around herself. "It's so cold."

"I know," Rory says. She unwraps a Cliff bar and gives it to her daughter. "Eat up, kid."

Sarah gives her a look. They both know the food is low. "What about you?" she asks.

"Eat," Rory answers.

Each time they get low on food, she maps out where they can find a town and stop for more. Each time, it's dangerous. So for now, she's rationing what they have left, knowing it won't last long.

For a moment, there is only the sound of Sarah's chewing. Then a shriek pierces the darkness. Human. The sound is far, far away. Still, Rory and Sarah both freeze, staring at each other. It lasts no more than a few seconds, but to them it goes on and on and on. When it stops, the silence is heavy and every hair on Rory's neck stands on end. *Crit or human attack?* She wonders.

She takes a deep breath, collecting herself, and squeezes Sarah's shoulder. "Let's go."

Sarah shimmies out of her sleeping bag and bundles it up in a flash. Then they quietly pack the tent and creep off into the dark.

. . .

The ground they walk on is frozen. Everywhere they look, the landscape is dead and dark. Any life that was once here is nearly gone. Some of the animals have survived the darkness, many have not—which gives them shitty odds even if Rory knew anything about hunting. The trees and leaves have slowly crumbled and decayed. After being deprived of light for so long, it's like they just gave up. The ponds, the lakes, and even most of the rivers are all frozen over, but there is never any snow. Just the bone-chilling cold and the gray waste stretching before them. Sometimes, Rory and Sarah make camp by the edge of a frozen lake—these are their favorite nights. When the moon is full and the stars twinkle from above, the ice seems to wink back at them, and things are almost normal. Then a scream in the distance, or the sound of heavy legs cutting through the forest splits through their little mirage, and they're forced to hunker down in the tent, waiting.

Sometimes they see others, most of the time they don't. Rory prefers the latter. When the world realized what was out there in the dark, and that the government had left them on their own, mankind descended into something rabid. At first, it happened slowly. A neighbor she'd known for years no longer said hello. A tension in the supermarket that was difficult to place. And then it sped up—almost happening overnight. It made her nauseous to think about what had become of humankind. It was like a sickness had taken hold—all the worst fears she'd had about society confirmed. There was no hope for the people left. And for a woman and a girl trekking alone across this barren wasteland, that was terrifying.

The world was full of monsters now, that was true. But most of them had human faces.

Thoughts like this always lead her back to that moment, years ago. She remembers Matt's face in her hands, the blood—

Stop, she says to herself. *Focus. Be here.* She'd let her thoughts travel too far. How long had she been in her own head? Quickly, she scans the surrounding forest, listening closely, hearing nothing.

And so they walk on.

. . .

"Mom?" Sarah asks when they lay awake in the tent that night.

"Yeah?"

"Do you ever miss your old friends?"

Sometimes the questions Sarah asks take Rory's breath away. Sarah had been young when they'd left, and sometimes Rory forgets she remembers any of their old life.

"Yeah," she says. "I do. Do you?"

Sarah smiles in the darkness. "I miss the barbecues and music. Uncle Nick and Aunt Susan."

Nick and Susan. Images of her wedding come into focus. They had both been there, smiling and laughing, all of them so young. All of them so without worry. She pushes the thought away.

"I also remember there being a lot of kids my age. I miss having other kids—well, even just other people around."

Rory exhales. Though she always anticipates these conversations, she still can't stand to have them.

"I know," Rory says. "But that life is over."

Sarah sighs, defeated. "Jesus. I know that, Mom," she whispers.

"I'm sorry," Rory says, feeling guilty immediately. "Sometimes it's just—I don't know, it's hard to see the point in thinking about it."

Sarah is quiet for so long that Rory thinks she's fallen

asleep. But then she whispers, "What do you think happened to them?"

Rory pauses for a moment. "I think they're gone, sweetie."

Sarah nods and says nothing more.

2072

Then

Rory

RORY AND MATT sat around a table in their basement with their closest friends, Nick and Susan, who lived next door. All that was visible was the outline of each other's faces in the dim light. While it was still daylight in their town—for now—they couldn't be caught having this conversation.

When the reports of crit attacks and disappearances sky-rocketed, the world had plunged into a panic. The president had declared Martial Law. Secret meetings were against the law. A curfew had been enforced. Neighbors turned on each other left and right. Things were coming to an end—that much was obvious.

"Nick, you sound insane, do you realize that?" Matt whispered. "This is *America*. They can't just—"

"Matt, you're not listening! Look around you, for fuck's sake!" Nick shouted. Susan put a hand on his arm. One look at her best friends was all Rory needed to remind herself that this fucked up world they were living in was real. Nick's eyes were wild, the bags under them suggested he hadn't slept in days. His hair was unruly, as was Susan's. They'd come to tell her and Matt something.

Rory didn't want to believe it, but somewhere inside, she knew it was true.

"I'm sorry," Nick whispered. "I'm sorry." He took a breath. "But it's true. Please, you can't go tomorrow."

"But they're saying it's the only way," Matt said. "They started colonizing Mars, what, fifty years ago? You've seen the videos. It's legit, Nick. And besides, what the fuck else can we do? Stay *here?*" he gestured around the room. "We have to think about Sarah. We've been waiting all year for our number to come up."

"I know, but—" Nick started.

"You want us to 'look around'?" Rory said calmly. "Look *outside,* Nick. Our time is running out. We have no other choice. The people are…it's not safe here. We'll be in full darkness in a matter of *months.*"

"You think we aren't thinking about our own children?" Susan whispered, looking at Rory. "You think we'd come to tell you this if it weren't real? Please. Don't go. Just listen to Nick."

"Just let me explain," Nick pleaded.

"Of course, man," said Matt, though not without agitation. "Go ahead."

"You know I told you they stopped all of our construction downtown about a year ago and had us start building the launch sites?" Nick began. "Everybody, everywhere in the States, immediately halted all other construction to work on these things."

Matt and Sarah nodded. Everyone knew about it—Operation Armageddon. In their lifetime, Earth had become doomed. Everyone had entered a lottery for a spot on a ship to Mars, which had tripled its colonization efforts. The odds were obvious: If your number was called, you lived. You got a new start, away from whatever the hell these *crits* were out there in the dark. If your number was not called, you were left here to die. There was no middle ground.

"And you've seen the launch site downtown—the one you guys are headed to tomorrow," Nick said. "It's massive. It fits thousands of people." He stopped and looked around, paranoia etched in every line of his face.

"Go on," Matt said.

"I was there a few days ago, and I shouldn't have been. But I wanted to see one of the ships take off—I remember when the government guys brought them in. They're impressive. And anyway, I made those security systems—I know my way past them," he looked at Susan, who nodded, urging him to go on. "So I kinda crept around because I knew there was a window in there, so I'd be able to see inside, and—" his voice broke.

"And what?" Matt pressed.

"Nobody's getting on those fucking ships, man," Nick said, eyes darting from person to person. "At least not any of us. Hundreds of people in there—all of them dressed in their best clothes with suitcases looking happy to be getting the hell out of here. These guys came in wearing full-on riot gear. They had gas masks on and...and before anyone could realize what was happening, all this yellow smoke started filling the air."

"What do you mean?" Rory whispered. But she knew.

"They gassed them. Parents, kids, everybody—they just started dropping. It was like some fucking Holocaust extermination. *I watched it.*"

Matt's hand tightened around Rory's. His mouth hung slightly open.

Nick was sweating now. "I just...I couldn't believe it.

The *screaming.* I mean, these were parents with little kids, old people…"

"Jesus Christ," Matt said.

"So I fucking *ran,* man," Nick went on. "I ran all the way home, and I was sure somebody was following me, but…nobody did."

Rory's brain was working a mile a minute. Surely this couldn't be true. This was the United States for Christ's sake. "Are you *sure—*"

"Rory, look at me," Nick said. His brow was covered in sweat, his hands were shaking. "*This* is at least part of why we're under Martial Law. There's not enough room on that fucking planet for all of us—I'd bet my life on it. Essentials and rich people only. If you go down there tomorrow, they're gonna kill you," he looked at both of them. His eyes pleading. "And they're gonna kill Sarah, too."

Rory pictured it for a second. They were already packed, just like Nick had said the other families were. She could see little Sarah standing there in her dress, looking up at them and smiling. She could see a line of government workers come in, each of them carrying masks. She couldn't make herself imagine the rest.

She looked at Matt. How could this be happening?

"So what are you guys going to do?" Matt asked quietly.

Nick and Susan exchanged a glance of despair. Their lottery number hadn't been called yet, anyway. Rory and Matt knew, ship or no ship, their friends' days were numbered.

"We have to try and make it in the dark," Nick said. "It's the only way that—"

There was a crash upstairs. They heard Sarah scream.

Matt was out of his chair in half a second, taking the

stairs by two. He opened the door at the top of the stairs and headed toward the sound of his daughter with Rory and their friends on his heels. They turned the corner in the living room and had barely enough time to register the scene—four armed men in uniforms and a woman in a white suit between them—before Matt nearly swallowed a fist to the face. Rory heard something in her husband's face *snap,* saw the blood rush from his nose, and watched him go down hard.

"Dad!" Sarah screamed and began to cry.

"Nick Fischer," the woman said with such unnerving nonchalance that Rory's stomach flipped. "After we checked *your* house, we thought you might be here."

"What—" Nick started, but Susan answered first.

"Where are our boys?" she asked.

"I'm Agent Pierce," the woman said, ignoring the question. "You're all coming with us."

"Where the fuck are my children?" Nick asked.

"Just outside," Pierce smiled, but barely. Rory would never forget that *smile,* how just one corner of her lip moved. Pierce stepped aside and through the screen in their front door, they saw Nick and Susan's children, Billy and Andrew, standing with another armed official. Pierce never took her eyes off the parents. "Take them," she said casually.

The men moved toward them at once.

"We're not going anywhere with—" Nick started, but he was cut off by a fist.

"Nick!" Susan screamed.

"Shut up," one of the officers said, binding her hands. Another one of them grabbed Rory.

"What the hell are you doing?" Matt said, his voice thick through the blood pouring out of his nose.

"As I said," Agent Pierce answered, "you're all coming."

All Rory heard was the sound of her daughter's screams. She looked at Matt, still defiant, though his face was smeared with blood. Inside, she felt her heart break to see him like that, but outside she stayed calm.

One of the officers grabbed Sarah's hand and started to drag her outside.

"Don't touch her!" Matt yelled, trying to stand. He was met with another fist that sent him to his knees. This time, he stayed there. The sight made Rory nauseous. A guard grabbed him under the shoulders and yanked him up.

"We done talking back now?" the guard said.

"Fuck you," Matt whispered, blood spattering from his mouth.

The guard laughed as he dragged Matt outside, the rest of them right behind.

The government had tried to keep some semblance of order as the world came crumbling down around them, but the evidence was everywhere. Crime had increased tenfold, garbage littered the streets, violent punishment awaited anyone who put a toe out of line. Rory would never forget that as she, her family, and her friends were loaded into the back of a van, bleeding and filthy with their hands bound, their neighbors watched in silence.

Agent Pierce and two of the officers sat in the back with them.

"Where are you taking us?" Nick asked.

Pierce just smiled, pristine in her white suit. Not a single hair out of place.

Her face was unforgettable. Sharp. Her eyes—befitting her name—were a piercing blue. Her short hair was ice blonde, her skin like wax, her lips thin, her brows and finger-nails perfectly groomed.

"Dad," Sarah said, her eyes rimmed with red. "I'm scared."

"I know, baby," Matt whispered. "It's gonna be okay."

Again, Pierce gave them that empty, thin-lipped smile.

Without even having to look out the front, Rory knew exactly where they were going. She was thinking fast.

"So what are you going to do then?" Nick said. Rory could see he knew where they were headed, too. "Kill every single person on earth?"

"We're not going to kill *everyone*," Pierce said. "We do have to recolonize somehow. But why would we take anyone but the best?"

"You're disgusting," Matt said.

"I'm making history," Pierce said, at last, an edge to her voice. "Did you *really* think we'd take 20 *billion* people? You can't be that stupid. The population has been out of control for decades, what we're doing solves more than just one problem. Future generations will read about what I've done."

Matt spat out a laugh. "Yeah," he said, "you're not wrong about that."

"Why do any of this?" Nick asked. "The lottery, all the preparation...why?"

Pierce scoffed at Nick like he was a child. "People needed something to hope for," she said. "Or we would've lost control a long time ago."

"The children," Susan said to Pierce, her voice barely a whisper. "Please."

Pierce smiled again. "As I said, we only have use for the *best*," she answered.

"And what does that mean, exactly?" Matt asked, blood

still dripping from his nose, soaking his shirt. "Anyone who paid millions?"

Again, the smile.

"Looks like it's gotten worse, Pierce," the driver said through the glass between them.

They all turned to look out the windshield. A huge crowd had gathered outside the launch area—some kind of protest was happening. The road was blocked. Something hit the side of the van, hard. They smelled gasoline. Rory felt her daughter lean closer to her.

"I want to go home," Sarah said, tears welling in her eyes.

"I know, baby," Rory said.

"What do you want me to do here?" the driver asked.

Without skipping a beat, Pierce answered. "Go through them."

Rory and Matt shared a glance. The driver slammed on the gas.

"No!" Rory shouted. But it was too late.

They heard the screams first. Then they felt a crunch underneath them. Then another. Then another.

Rory closed her eyes.

"Mom!" Sarah shrieked. "Mom! Mom!"

2076

Now

RORY

"Mom," Sarah whispers, shaking her. "Mom, wake up."

Rory's eyes snap open. Her left taking a fraction of a second longer.

"What is it? What's wrong?" she whispers back into the darkness.

"There's something out there," Sarah says, looking at one side of the tent.

And then she hears it. Footsteps crunching the leaves. Not quickly, but steadily. And getting closer. Whatever it is, it will be on them soon.

Rory grabs a rifle and crawls to the door of the tent.

"Don't open it," Sarah whispers, the first tinge of fear in her voice.

"I have to, baby," Rory says, looking back. "If anything happens, tell me the plan."

"Mom, please don't," Sarah says, putting a hand on Rory's arm. Her grip is tight. Terrified.

"Sarah," Rory says, setting down the gun and putting both hands on her daughter's shoulders. The footsteps are closer. *Crunch, crunch. Crunch, crunch. Crunch, crunch.* Is there more than one set? "Tell me what you're going to do if I don't come back."

Sarah has tears in her eyes, but swallows hard and blinks them away. She hesitates, but only for a moment. "I wait," she says. "If it comes toward the tent, I shoot. Then I grab the emergency bag and run, find a safe place and hide. Then I—" her voice breaks. "I keep going north."

Rory nods. There's a smaller bag inside her own that holds essential equipment only. Sarah's resourceful enough to restock what she needs when she's safe, if it comes to that. There was a time in the beginning when Rory knew she had to stay alive—Sarah wouldn't survive without her. But now, while it still scares her, she knows Sarah would make it on her own. They've been through enough to prove that.

"It's gonna be okay," Rory says. "Just wait and listen." The footsteps are closing in. Fifty yards.

She kisses her daughter once on the head, picks up her gun, and opens the tent. Inside, Sarah kneels down in the corner, her gun trained on the door as Rory zips it closed behind her.

The moon is barely visible, but there is enough light to illuminate the shadows coming toward them. They trudge across the dead valley, two dark spots on a gray canvas.

She lifts her rifle and gets them in her sights, her left eye drooping slightly to one side. If she takes a shot, it needs to be a good one.

One of the figures is big and one is small. The big one stops, and with cat-like quickness pushes the small one behind them and draws their own pistol, pointing it directly at Rory.

"Why are you walking towards this tent?" Rory asks, her voice and rifle steady.

The shape doesn't speak for a moment. The silence stretches between them. Rory's finger is light on the trigger, one quick pull will do it.

"We saw it," a man's voice. Rory's blood freezes. *Shit.* "We thought if it were abandoned there might be some food left."

The little one pokes their head out from behind the man. Rory can tell that it's a child. The man pushes it back.

"We're about to run out ourselves," Rory says. "We can't help you. Move on."

"Please," the man says. The tone of his voice makes Rory pause. In it, she hears something beyond desperation: an exhaustion she knows all too well. "My boy...we're starving." He holsters his pistol and raises his arms, showing her he won't use it.

"I said we can't help you," Rory answers, still ready to pull the trigger if he reaches for that gun.

"I promise you," the man said. "We mean no harm."

Then they hear it.

A distant shuffling, that same chittering sound that has haunted Rory's dreams since childhood. Something else is approaching now. The man and his son are still about thirty yards away, but she can nearly feel the blood drain out of them.

"Please," the man says, voice shaking.

She has no more than a few seconds to make a decision. She can see the boy shivering behind the man—cold, hungry, and now terrified.

"Let them in, Mom!" Sarah whispers from behind her. Rory turns to see the tent flap open and her daughter's head poking out.

"I told you to—"

"For God's sake, Mom! He has a kid. Let them in!"

"Jesus Christ," Rory mutters, hoping against hope she doesn't regret what she says next. "Come on, then!" she says to the man, lowering her gun and waving them toward her. "Move your asses. Now!"

In one fluid motion, the man turns, lifts the child, and runs toward Rory. He is faster than he looks, and stronger.

Rory runs back the short distance to the tent and looks at her daughter.

"Don't you *ever*—" she starts, but Sarah cuts her off.

"What if that were you and me?" she says, "after that night at the lake house?"

Rory looks away, back at the man and his son, knowing her daughter has a point, praying they made the right call.

Rory sticks her head out of the tent, the chittering is getting louder now, but she still can't see the crit. The child and the man are only a few yards away now.

"Move!" she whispers. "Come on, MOVE."

They reach the tent and dive inside, both of them covered so fully in layers that really, only the child's bright eyes against dark skin are visible.

She zips up the tent, which is barely covered by a stand of small trees, and they wait.

Finally, the sound closes in. The leaves crunching under several spindly legs is unmistakable, the chittering sound even more so. It shuffles along the frozen ground, searching. Getting closer.

She holds her rifle pointed at the tent entrance. Her hands don't shake. The four of them sit frozen. Waiting.

They watch its shadow cross in front of the tent. Six spider-like legs stick out from its sinewy body at odd angles. Its enormous head whips back and forth, sniffing. Rory knows it knows they're here. They hear its jaw, filled with hundreds of razor-sharp teeth, snap shut just inches away. Nothing but the sheet-like tent wall between them. Rory's heart hammers in her chest, loud enough that she's sure the crit can hear it. She smells urine and can't tell if it is her own. She follows its silhouette with her rifle. It's *right there.* It's going to find them. *Be ready,* she tells herself with a steadying breath. *Be ready.*

Suddenly, there is a long, distant scream. Miles away, they know, but in a dark, silent world, the sound carries.

Just as she had at ten years old, Rory *feels* the crit's hunger as it turns toward the sound. The next second, it's gone.

They wait what feels like hours, but Rory knows it is only moments, before they let out a collective sigh of relief. Finally, Rory turns to study her new companions.

The man and his son huddle together in a far corner of the tent. The boy's eyes are huge, lantern-bright, and staring, but he is as calm as a frozen lake. The man drew his gun when the crit approached, Rory sees, but he lowers it as soon as they make eye contact.

"Who the hell are you?" Rory says.

"Thank you," he whispers, and then he collapses.

2072

Then

SAM

"I'M HOME!" Sam called as he walked in the door. Since leaving the army, he'd been teaching a few criminology courses at Florida State College. But even those had become less and less frequent in the last year, as the world around them grew darker.

He'd begun the semester with a class list of two hundred students. He was now down to fifty-six.

"In the living room," Becca called from down the hall. She, like the rest of the United States, had been glued to the television for nearly a year.

Becca had lost her job in advertising six months ago. Or rather, her agency—like many—had simply gone under as their clients' businesses had gone under. Shortly after, so did the entire economy. Sam only continued going to work for a sense of purpose, but he knew that sooner rather than later, that would come to an end as well. His checks were sporadic these days; sometimes he'd go weeks without getting paid. Sometimes it wasn't even through the school, and instead, his students paid him in resources—food, matches, the always-coveted beer—which was fine with him, since money was becoming more useless every day. He was cursed with the Achilles heel of all teachers: caring too much about his students. But now it was just a question of who would stop showing up first—him or them? Things on the outside were spiraling out of control, and it was getting too dangerous to even leave the house some days.

Sam kicked off his shoes and set down his briefcase. He turned around and snapped all five padlocks into their bolts, then propped the barricade bar against the door. It didn't matter how many politicians had campaigned to wage the "law and order" war—when the world went to shit, so did the law. That was evident from his commute home every day. More stores vandalized, more buildings in ruin. He used to enjoy his commute to work. He'd leave early in the morning and listen to an audiobook or music on his leisurely stroll through downtown Jacksonville, usually stopping at his favorite coffee shop for a latte and a bagel before catching up on grading papers. But those days were long gone. He would never risk putting in headphones anymore, and his firearm was always strapped to his waistband, just in case.

When things had started to shift, the first thing he'd noticed was the cold. While they were still in daylight, the approaching darkness brought freezing temperatures with it. He'd been scavenging sites for winter clothing for himself and Becca, just in case, which had cost him a fortune in both money and resources. But after a life spent in extreme heat, the chill in the air felt strangely ominous. When they'd learned what was out there, they had their confirmation.

Things had started small once there was an uptick in crit attacks. Petty crime went up—robbery, assault, trespassing. But when the attacks increased, along with the news that the darkness was expanding more rapidly, there had been a distinct shift in human nature. Murder, home invasion, and violent crime had skyrocketed. He'd use it for his curriculum if it weren't so damn terrifying.

"Hey honey," he said, joining Becca on the couch and cracking open two beers. Payment from a student this week.

"Hey," she sighed, turning away from the news to take a beer from him. "Same shit, different day."

The screen showed an image of Boston. It was completely dark now. Helicopters flew overhead with spotlights, illuminating the carnage below. Crits ran wild across the screen in dark, horrifying blurs.

He still remembers the chaos back when the first images of the crits had gone public. The UN had tried to take them out at first, but it was impossible. No matter what they did, the crits just seemed to multiply.

Sam never knew his mom, and his father had passed away seven years ago, but Becca's parents lived in Salem, MA. About six months ago, Becca and Sam had urged them to pack their bags, get in the car, and drive down to Florida, which still remained in the sunlight. It was like pulling teeth, but finally, they'd agreed. However, the day before they were set to leave, they stopped answering their phones. Becca had tried their neighbors nearby, but their calls all went to voicemail. They'd never heard from her parents again.

Something had changed in Becca after that. Sam always thought it was the not knowing, the lack of closure that she just couldn't reconcile.

"We have to start making a real plan," Becca said quietly as a crit leapt from one building to another on screen.

Sam sighed, "I know," he said, squeezing her hand.

They'd entered the lottery over a year ago. It was time to

be realistic. Their number wasn't coming up. And even if it did, Sam wasn't sure it was safe, anyway.

He had spent enough time in the army to know that whatever plan was in place for the survival of the human race, it didn't end well for most of the population. One way or another, they'd have to try and make it on their own, in the dark.

But at what cost?

Now

Rory

Hours later, the stranger stirs.

By now, Rory has gone through all of the new arrivals' things and realized how desperate they must be. They carry almost no food, and she knew whatever food they'd had, this man had likely given to the boy. It's what Rory would've done. The man is clearly starving and thirsty. They'd bundled him in a sleeping bag they'd found in his backpack and waited.

They have so little to spare, but Sarah keeps insisting they let them stay. The tent is already warming up with the body heat from two new arrivals, and for that small thing, Rory is grateful. But the unease she feels at this strange man's presence is nauseating.

The man finally cracks open an eye, and Rory watches panic consume him. He is immediately alert, groping blindly for his gun.

"It's alright," she says, "we're not going to hurt you. Who are you?" Rory realizes how ragged she must look to these strangers. Her poorly buzzed hair has started to grow back in uneven patches, scars poking through where she'd cut herself shaving it off. She and Sarah only sponge bathe when they can afford to use water for bathing instead of drinking, which isn't often. Their last wash was weeks ago. Rory's face—marred by the huge scar that stretches from eyebrow to chin, made by a knife that had nearly taken her eye—is pale and gaunt from hunger. She hasn't changed her clothes in months.

Slowly, the man seems to realize where he is, what's happened. The boy huddles close to him. The whole time the man had been asleep, the boy had never once let go of his arm, and he hasn't said a word yet. Rory knows they'll only get answers from this man.

"Who are you?" Rory asks again, handing him her canteen full of water.

The man stares at her, his brown eyes looking at her with both gratitude and suspicion. "I'm Sam," he says, taking a sip of the water. "And this is Jacob. We're nearly out of food, we've been hungry for days. When we saw your tent...we had no other choice," he sighs. "I'm sorry—I know how scary it must be for us to show up out of nowhere."

Rory looks at him but doesn't answer.

"Thank you," he adds, lifting the canteen. "For the water, and for...earlier."

Rory nods. "Where are you from?"

"We started in Florida," he says.

"What are you doing this far north?" she asks.

"I could ask you the same," Sam says.

Rory's eyes narrow. "We're not the ones depending on you for help," she says, shifting her pistol.

Sam looks at the boy, who gives nothing away, then sighs again. "Point taken. We heard the broadcast," he answers.

Rory nods again.

"Can we…stay for a day or two?" Sam asks. "Just to get our strength back. Then we'll get out of your way."

Rory almost laughs. People are dangerous, it's just the way it is. She doesn't like this. She doesn't know them.

"No," she says.

"I realize this must be scary for you," Sam responds. "I'm not…I—" he digs through his bag, taking a picture out. "I had a wife," he says. "She…"

He hands the picture to Rory. It's a photo of him—younger, healthier, and in the daylight. He has long dreads that go past his shoulders, which have long since been shaved, and his arm around a beautiful woman. Despite her fear, Rory's heart tightens.

"What happened to her?" she asks.

He's quiet for a long moment before he looks up at her, his eyes lingering on her scar. "People," he says.

She nods, understanding. There's something in his eyes that tells her he's sincere.

"Come on, Mom," Sarah whispers from across the tent. "Just let them stay."

Sam turns to Sarah and then looks pleadingly at Rory. His dark skin has taken on a gray undertone, most likely from exhaustion. But still—she can't stave off the fear.

"We would never hurt you," he says.

She thinks about it—how desperate Sarah is to be around other people. She looks at Jacob, who sits silently next to his father. He is so small and so afraid. She thinks about that night at the lake, how terrified Sarah had been after.

"Fine," she sighs. "Two days."

Sam smiles. And even Jacob, who has remained completely still, relaxes. He crawls into Sam's sleeping bag, and tucks himself against him.

"But I'm keeping these while you're with us," she says, raising the guns and a hunting knife she'd found in Sam's things.

"Of course," Sam says. "And thank you."

She looks at Jacob, who looks hungry, and takes out some jerky to give to him. He wolfs it down greedily in seconds, and she softens. This poor kid. He smiles up at her in thanks and tucks himself back into Sam. Without another word, they're both asleep.

"You're okay with this?" Rory whispers to Sarah as she climbs into her own sleeping bag.

"Yes," Sarah says. "They seem okay to me."

Rory sighs. "We can't trust them yet."

"I know."

"You sleep first," Rory says.

"Okay."

Sarah is asleep immediately, as always, but Rory lies awake. In a few hours, she'll wake her daughter and try to get some sleep herself, but for now she decides to let her sleep. Let her mind take her elsewhere. Let her live, for a few hours, somewhere better than this existence in the dark.

Let her dream of sunlight.

. . .

The next morning, Sarah chats away to Jacob, who smiles warily, but still never makes a sound. Rory's head is clearer after a few hours of sleep. She didn't mind last night's watch, she never sleeps well anymore anyway.

"You're up," Sam says.

By now, Sam has taken off his outer layers and is dressed in a too-big flannel shirt, jeans, and wool socks. His hair is cropped short like hers, his skin is impossibly smooth, and his brown eyes are alert. Rory can see the outline of muscle beneath his flannel.

"I'm up," she says. "How'd you sleep?"

"Great," Sam answers. He looks like he's gained some strength back. "Thank you, again."

Rory nods and sinks back into her pillow, trying to figure out what to do. It is getting darker, she knows. In a day or two, the moon will be only a sliver, making it too dangerous to move. Then, she knows, it will be fully dark for two days. No moon at all. And now they have two strangers with them.

"Can I talk to you?" Sam asks, pulling Rory out of her thoughts.

"Sure."

"Outside," Sam nods toward the tent opening.

Rory looks at Sarah, who gives her a thumbs up.

"Okay," she says, making a show of picking up her pistol before leaving the tent.

. . .

Outside, the approaching new moon is evident. The minimal light is fading, it seems, by the second. Rory knows that Sam is clocking it, too. She can see her breath in the waning moonlight and feel the cold in the roots of her teeth. Yet—even though she almost feels guilty for it—she still can't help taking in the beauty of where they made camp. They are standing in the clearing now, and the frozen earth is still and silent under the crescent moon. For a moment, it could seem like nothing was wrong in the world. Like maybe they'd just gone for a long camping trip.

For a moment.

Sam and Rory walk away from the tent until they think they're far enough away where they won't be heard, then Sam turns to face her.

"We're not strong enough to travel yet," he says gently. "I know you and Sarah are good people. That much is…obvious." He looks out across the clearing, mulling over his next words. Then he turns back. "I know you don't know us. I don't want to take advantage of your kindness. But I don't want to put my son at risk, either. Can we stay with you through the new moon? I promise you, I'll show you we're good. We're not like…the others that are left."

Rory doesn't answer for a moment. Part of her knew this was coming, and she's pissed off.

"How the hell am I supposed to know that?" she snaps. "I have a daughter to think about here."

Sam's gaze is steady. "And I have a son," he says. "Who's exhausted, malnourished, and terrified."

Rory feels a pang of guilt. Jacob is just a child, too. Her one weak spot.

"I was a teacher before this," Sam says. "I'm trustworthy. I…" he reaches into his pocket and pulls out a wallet. It's so strange to see it—like something from another life.

"Here," he says. "I don't even know how I still have this, but this was my faculty ID."

Rory takes it. Samuel Nielson, criminology professor.

"It *looks* legit," she says.

"I promise," he says. "You can trust us."

She knows, somewhere deep, that they can. And it's unlikely that they'd be a burden or slow them down—she remembers last night. How quickly Sam picked up Jacob and ran toward them. And even through total exhaustion, he'd been ready to fight. Ready to kill. He'd stayed calm, cool, and collected when it mattered most. *And...Rory thinks...so had the boy*. He couldn't be more than nine or ten, and he hadn't even screamed. Hadn't given them away at all. His huge eyes had just stared.

"We barely have enough food for ourselves," Rory says.

"Exactly. You need us," Sam answers.

"What?"

"You're running out of food every day," Sam says. "And if we don't come across any towns, we'll have to hunt."

"'We?'"

"I used to hunt. Before. And I was in the army for a while," at this, Sam studies Rory for some kind of response. She gives none. "You need us just as much as we need you," he finishes.

Rory thinks about this. Was he telling the truth? She thinks again about last night. She thinks about her daughter.

"Army," Rory says. "You know how to fight?"

Sam stares at her for a long moment. "Yes." Then before Rory can even ask, he says, "I can teach her."

"Then we have a deal," Rory says. She reaches out her hand.

Finally, Sam's face betrays a smile. "Thank you," he answers, and shakes Rory's hand.

. . .

"Sam and Jacob are going to stay with us for a while," Rory says to Sarah when they get back. "Is that okay?"

Sarah smiles, and Rory's heart breaks. She misses having people around so much, Rory knows. "Of course," Sarah says. "It's great. Thanks, Mom."

Rory nods. "It's going to be a new moon in about a day," she says. "We have enough food for now, but…"

"I know," Sarah says. "He was good. Last night, I mean. And he can hunt."

Rory's eyebrows come together. "How did—"

"We're in a clearing," Sarah says, rolling her eyes. "Sound carries. Sam was right. We do need them."

Rory chuckles. "Yeah, we do," she says. "It's settled then. But if anything they do makes you even slightly uncomfortable—"

"I know, Mom," Sarah says.

"I know you do, honey," Rory says, rubbing her scar. "That's why I'm asking you to say something if you need to."

"I will, Mom. Promise."

Rory nods, hoping like hell she's making the right call.

They spend their last evening before the new moon chatting with their guests in the tent. They only learn the bare minimum about Sam and Jacob, but still, Rory has to admit to herself, it's nice to have company. For one night, it seems things are almost okay. She has a sliver of hope. Would Sarah grow up in a world with other people? Is there a chance, even without sunlight, for something better? She falls asleep thinking, for the first time in a long time, about hope.

2073

Then

Jacob

"So how did your first lesson go?" Paul asked excitedly as they walked home together. Paul lived right next door and was a few years ahead of Jacob in school. Their parents had always been friends, so the two of them grew up like brothers. Paul always included him even though Jacob was younger.

Jacob looked down. Class hadn't gone well, but he was nervous to say so to Paul.

"Oh, I know that look," Paul said, before Jacob can answer. "That bad, huh?"

Jacob snapped his head up. "I couldn't do anything!" he wailed. He could feel the tears coming on. He'd held them back the whole day since class this morning.

"Hey! It's okay, come here," Paul said, wrapping him in a hug. He took Jacob's shoulders and looked into his eyes. "It's normal for that to happen in the first few classes. This is all brand new right now and you're just learning how to do it."

Jacob sniffled, not convinced. "But the other kids got the hang of it by the end," he said. "What if I never do?"

Paul smiled. "I couldn't figure it out in my first few classes, either, you know," he said.

"Really?" Jacob said. Maybe there *was* hope after all.

"Really," said Paul. "It takes time. You'll get it."

"Okay," Jacob said, feeling a little better.

"You know what always helps though?" Paul asked.

"What?"

"That special dessert your mom makes. Did she tell you we're coming over for dinner tonight?"

This was the best news ever. Jacob loved getting to hang out with Paul—he was so cool. "You are?" he asked.

"We are. And we can get some practice in if you want."

Jacob smiled, wiping away the last of his tears. "Thank you," he said.

"You got it, buddy," Paul said.

. . .

Dinner that night was great. Jacob loved Paul's parents almost as much as he loved his own. They stayed for hours, long after dinner had finished, telling stories and laughing late into the night. Jacob was getting bored and his butt was sore from the chair.

He finally got up and tapped Paul on the shoulder.

"Can we go practice my lessons?" he asked.

Paul smiled. "Absolutely."

The two boys got up and headed into the other room. The door was almost shut when they heard Paul's dad.

"Did you hear about Will?" Paul's dad asked from the other room.

"We heard," Jacob's dad responded. "Horrible. It's getting worse."

Jacob started to open the door to ask what they were talking about, but Paul put a hand on his shoulder. When

Jacob looked up at him, Paul had a finger to his lips. *Be quiet.*

"And the darkness gets closer every day now," Jacob's mom said. "We can all see it."

"What about your boss? Gabe, right?" Paul's mother asked. "Does he still have some kind of plan?"

"He does," Jacob's mom answered, then corrected herself. "We all do. It's tricky, you know, hard to talk about it at work, but…"

"We're running out of time," Jacob heard his dad say. "Gabe knows that."

"I just…" Paul's dad said. "The kids."

"I know," Jacob's mom answered. "They're the priority. Always."

Jacob had been able to sense something going on for a long time. He'd always lived in a world that was constant sunlight, but lately, things were changing. It was colder. He kept hearing whispers about people disappearing. People had been acting strange. And the teachers in his class seemed more tense than usual.

He looked up at Paul, who started out at his parents. When he glanced down at Jacob, he transformed his face into a kind smile. But Jacob hadn't missed the look on his face just moments before.

Fear.

2074

Then

Sam

"What was that?" Becca whispered.

The sound had made Sam's heart catapult into his chest, but he didn't want to freak Becca out any more than she already was.

"I'm not sure," he said. "But it's okay. Nothing's getting by those padlocks."

Becca scoffed. "Have you seen the news in Boston? We need to start moving our stuff upstairs."

He knew she was right. So many people had left the upstairs apartments—whether to get on a ship or try and make it on foot, they had no idea. But Sam had taken a trip up to the twentieth floor the other day just to check it out, and it was all but deserted.

"It's getting so fucking *cold*," Becca said. Sam could see her breath even inside the apartment now. They were constantly bundled, and though Sam was worried about someone seeing the smoke, they wouldn't survive without a fire going. He'd put blackout curtains over every window in the house and had barricaded them as well as he could with two-by-fours. But still, every moment they lived in fear.

"I know," he said. "Walking up to the twentieth should warm us up at least, though," he laughed. Becca didn't.

The darkness had overtaken them a few weeks ago. When it was getting noticeable, Sam had set a boundary line outside in the street to measure how quickly it was closing in.

It had surpassed the boundary in a matter of days.

"There it is again!" Becca said, louder this time.

"Shhh," Sam said. "I heard it too."

A scattering of legs running through the parked cars outside. Even having seen the footage in the northeast, Sam still couldn't wrap his head around it.

"Where are you going?" Becca asked, reaching out for him as he stood up.

"I'm just gonna go make sure the windows are all closed," Sam lied. He knew the windows were closed. "Stay here, and stay quiet. I'll be right back."

He tiptoed toward the kitchen window, where he'd heard the sound coming from. Each creak of the floorboards set him on edge. Slowly, as quietly as possible, he closed the door to the living room, plunging himself into total darkness in the kitchen. He waited there, focusing on his breathing, letting his eyes adjust. After about thirty seconds he could see the shapes around him—the pots and pans, the island counter, the kitchen sink.

And then he heard it. A *chittering*. Then the sound of someone moaning, just beyond the wall of the kitchen.

Moving toward the window, he held up a shaking hand to pull back the blind. One centimeter. Two.

Whoosh.

Something enormous and hairy flew past. Sam dropped

the curtain, flattening himself against the wall and grinding his teeth together to keep from screaming.

What the fuck *was that?*

But he knew. He slowed his breathing, trying to get his heart rate under control. *You've already seen it,* he told himself. *Just look.*

He slowly, carefully lifted the blind a second time and peered out.

The moon was full that night and seemed to set a spotlight on them. "Crits" was what the news had called them. The repulsive, spidery creatures that inhabited the darkness. He could see them outside the window—several of them, maybe three or four—huddled over the body of a flailing man. Feeding.

They'd torn his entire chest apart, but he was still alive. His legs kicked out wildly, still trying to fight off his attackers as they ate him alive. Sam squeezed his fists to try to keep from vomiting. In the moonlight, he could see the crits' legs were veiny with muscle. The claws on their arachnid feet razor-sharp. Their victim gargled his final screams and then fell silent.

"Oh my God," he heard Becca whisper behind him, making him jump again.

"Becca," he said, dropping the blind. "I'm sorry...I didn't want to scare you."

"Scare me?" she asked, incredulous. "I'm fucking scared, Sam. You can't shield me from what's out there," she pointed to the window with a shaking hand.

"I know," he said. The scene outside had jolted him. He looked at his wife. "We have to move upstairs tonight."

He could no longer pretend that they'd be safe from the

outside world on the first floor. The crits were here. And no amount of padlocks would save them.

. . .

The first few weeks in the twentieth-floor apartment were awful. Even stories above, they couldn't escape the sound of the horrors below. The screaming. The gunfire. The crits shuffling and climbing and screeching. Thankfully, the crits hadn't blown out any of the windows, but judging from the footage they'd seen of Boston, it wasn't impossible.

After those first few weeks, the city grew silent. The last reports they'd heard were so shocking that neither he nor Becca wanted to believe them, but deep down, he knew they were true. Only certain people had made it onto the ships. For everyone else, the lottery number had been a death sentence. Sam had always had the suspicion that it was a bunch of bullshit, but the weight of that reality was another thing entirely. They were on their own.

"We'll try to provide radio updates when we can," said the last remaining news anchor on CNN, who'd stared into the camera disheveled, eyes rimmed with red. "But this is our final television broadcast. God be with you."

Someone at the network must've then put sitcoms on autoplay, because those ran for a few days until everything turned to static. Sam always felt thankful to whoever did that. It must've been how all the passengers on the *Titanic* felt when the band kept playing.

A few days after the sitcoms stopped, everything went out. Sam and Becca had stockpiled essentials in the weeks leading up to the grid outage. Their trips to the stores had become less frequent as the world descended into madness. They didn't have enough to last forever, but they had enough to last for now.

"We have to try not to panic," he whispered to Becca in bed one night. "We're going to be okay." They both pretended to believe it.

. . .

Since the grid had gone dark, the elevators didn't work anymore, which made them feel a bit safer—who the hell would want to climb twenty floors? But still, they kept the deadbolts locked in the new apartment and barricaded the door at night. One other person had come to the same conclusion as them and moved to the twentieth floor. His name was Chet, a sixty-year-old man who'd retired from Wisconsin to Jacksonville a few years back after his wife died. They often shared meals and glasses of whatever booze they'd been able to stow away, chatting about what might come next. What they regretted. What they would've done differently. The thoughts that only plague you when you know your life is coming to an end.

In a backwards way, those first few months they spent in the apartment—when the city below was finally silent—were some of the best times of Sam's life. They ate canned food, read by candlelight, danced to no music, and talked until they lost track of how many hours had passed. Time meant nothing and everything at once. The Collapse, as the news had started calling it, had made them acutely aware of their own mortality, and while they were together, he and Becca were determined not to waste their final days. They were prisoners in their own apartment, and yet they'd never been so free.

"Well, this isn't exactly how I pictured the rest of my retirement," Chet said one night, sipping on a scotch he'd found in one of the other abandoned apartments.

"Well, *we* hadn't expected to retire for several more years," Becca laughed.

"I'm just glad you two stayed." Chet smiled sadly, eyes crinkling above his mostly-white beard. Chet was a die-hard fitness junkie with free weights he'd carried all the way up to his new apartment on the twentieth floor. Despite living on canned non-perishables, he was still lean and strong.

He leaned forward, chin resting on thick forearms, and turned serious. "And even though I'm glad you stayed," he said, "you can't stay here forever. I know you heard that broadcast, same as I did."

Sam and Becca looked at each other. It was true. The broadcast had come through a few days ago, offering refuge in Calgary with a chance at escape.

"We heard it," Sam said.

"But how can we even know it's real?" said Becca.

"You can't," Chet answered. "But you have to go anyway."

Sam had thought the same thing, but Becca disagreed. They'd argued about it all week. Deep down, he didn't really want to leave. But their supplies got lower every day. And what they were doing—this wasn't a life. This was existing within four walls.

"What about you?" Becca looked at Chet, getting heated. "Are you going to up and leave for Canada?"

"Shit, no," he said. "But I'm old. And I'm tired."

Becca set her chin. "If you're not going, we're not going either," she answered.

Chet smiled, finished the last of his drink and nodded. "Well, it'll be nice to have company while we starve to death, at least," he said.

"Exactly," Becca said, smiling weakly.

. . .

Over the next few days, they didn't bring it up, though every time Sam turned on their little battery-powered radio, he heard that same voice.

"Can anyone hear me? My name is Gabe. Today is May 17th. I'm broadcasting from Calgary, Canada, where we have found ships left from the Mars recolonization attempt."

He allowed himself to imagine it. Safety. A chance at a new life. Boarding a ship and setting off to a new planet, a new future.

If any of it was real.

One afternoon, he and Becca sat on the couch reading. They were running out of new books, even after scouring the apartments on their floor and several below, and soon he'd have to start re-reading, which he was dreading. He knew he needed to bring up the broadcast to her again, he just didn't know how.

There was a knock on the door.

"Open up, it's Chet," he heard from the other side.

Sam looked through the hole and unlocked all 5 deadbolts, opening the door to Chet's large silhouette leaning against the doorframe.

Chet examined his fingernails for a moment while he leaned. "Oh, what the hell," he said, looking up. "I could use one last adventure. I'll go."

Sam smiled. Clapping his friend on the shoulder. He turned to Becca.

"What do you think?" he said.

Becca looked around the apartment and smiled sadly. "Well God forbid you fall and break a hip," she said. "Just what we need is you coming back to haunt us. We'll go, too."

Chet laughed. "Okay, kids," he said. "Pack your bags. We leave in two days."

2076 — EVE OF THE NEW MOON

Now

SAM

SAM FEELS LIKE HE'S LIVED IN FEAR for as long as he can remember, and that isn't something he can let go of easily. It isn't him. If what happened a few days ago hadn't happened, they would've never ended up in this position. He knows that most of the people left are far worse than the crits. Those thoughts creep in often. *How could you have brought Jacob here? You don't know these people, it isn't safe.*

"Still awake?" Rory whispers, making him jump. "Sorry," she smiles.

"No, it's me," he answers. "Jumpy these days."

"I get it," she answers. "You don't have to worry about us."

"I know," he says. And he does. "I could say the same to you, but since you're still up, I doubt you'd believe me."

"You'd be correct."

He smiles. "You two aren't like most of the freaks left out there," he says after a while. "Have you…run into people much?"

"From time to time."

"That scar…" he starts, before he can help himself.

"A story for another day," she says.

They're quiet for a long time, but he can tell that she's still awake, so he asks, "What made you follow the broadcast?"

She scoffs. "What made *you?*"

"At first, necessity. Now…" he thinks. "Now, mainly it's just for something to do. Give the kid hope, you know," he nods toward Jacob, who's fast asleep.

Rory softens. "I can understand that," she answers quietly, looking at Sarah.

"Do you think it's real?" he asks.

"Do I think what's real?"

"The safe house from the broadcast. The ships. The people. All of it."

"Honestly?" she sighs. "No."

His heart sinks. Most days, he doesn't either.

"But if there's even a chance," Rory continues, "we have to try. For them."

And Sam knows she's right. It's the only reason he's kept going. If the wrong people found Jacob…

Don't think about it, he forces himself to stop. *We'll be careful.*

Army life trained him well. Not just to fight and kill, if necessary, but it had given him unparalleled instincts for people. And for the first time in a long time, he could sleep for more than twenty minutes at a time around strangers. They're good people. He knows it.

"You can get some sleep," he says. "You don't have anything to fear from me."

"You're a man," she whispers. "Of course I do."

2072

Then

Rory

Rory stumbled as a guard shoved her out of the van and into a long hallway, her friends and all the kids right behind her. The fluorescent lights above them flickered, and they could just hear the noise of a crowd somewhere up ahead, confirming their worst fear: they were being sent to board a ship that would never come. Nick's response was physical, he was shaking like a leaf standing next to Rory, whose mind was moving a mile a minute as it switched from disbelief to fury, panic just below the surface. The armed guards were all around them, each step made the hallway feel smaller and the crowd sound louder up ahead. There was no way out. *We have to do something,* she knew. But what?

Her daughter looked up at her. "I'm scared, Mom."

"I know, baby," she said. "It's gonna be okay."

Ahead of them, Pierce smiled.

"Where are we going?" Susan asked, though they all already knew.

"You're in luck!" Pierce said. "Turns out your lottery number came up, too."

"You evil bitch—" Susan started, but one of the soldiers hit her hard between the shoulder blades with the butt of his rifle. She cried out, stumbling awkwardly as she tried to protect herself with her zip-tied hands. The boys screamed.

"HEY!" Nick shouted, lunging at the soldier. Matt shouldered him as Rory helplessly watched Susan struggle to her feet.

"They'll kill all of us," Matt whispered. "Shut up."

The sound of the crowd built, people chattering happily, thinking they were getting on a ship to start a new life away from this dying planet.

Finally, they reached a set of double doors and Pierce turned to them.

"Cut them loose," she said to her men.

The men cut their zip ties one by one and pushed the doors open, dumping them into the crowd. Hundreds of people had been herded in like sheep. They were the only ones without luggage, the only ones in casual clothing. The only ones bleeding. Everyone else was dressed in their best for the adventure they would never take.

"Enjoy your trip," Pierce said, smiling.

"Fuck you," Rory spat.

Once more, Pierce gave them that terrible, empty grin. Then she turned and left, leaving them there in the crowd.

2072

Then

Pierce

Fucking Nick Fischer, she thinks as she watches the door slam in their faces.

To be fair, he wasn't the only one who'd figured it out. Hence the lynch mob they'd just massacred outside the stadium. He was just another fly she'd had to swat this morning while Armageddon officially went tits up.

When the DHS and STRATCOM had approached her to lead Armageddon years ago, it had been the best day of her life. If she'd been able to feel things like most people, she may have even cried. But most of the time, she felt nothing, except for the occasional rage.

Which is precisely why she'd been selected.

They needed someone who could stomach decisions that most couldn't. Her Captain had told her that the plan needed to include an element of hope for the masses. Otherwise, the chaos would've started long before now. But rats like Nick Fischer were the reason the plan was starting to break. She had a contingency plan for herself, of course. In fact, today was her turn to kiss this festering wound of a planet good-bye. But this morning, her Captain had told her not to show

61

up until *after* she'd dealt with the Fischers. He'd been furious that she'd let him slip through the night before they were set to leave, and he didn't give a shit if she made their departure time or not.

And now she was late.

"Move your ass, Tom," she said to her first-in-command security guard. "We need to get the fuck over to base. Now."

"Copy," he said, jogging up ahead of her. When they reached the exit door where they'd just come in, Tom stopped her. There was no window, but they could hear the sounds of the crowd beyond.

"We can't know how bad it is out there," Tom said.

"We just came through this way," Pierce responded icily. "We had to have mowed down half the crowd. We'll be fine." She pulled out a pistol from her hip holster. Turned off the safety. Reached for the door.

"Boss," Tom said, staying her hand. "I don't like this," it wasn't like Tom to hesitate.

"Jesus, Tom," she said. "Get a fucking grip." She pushed open the door.

The mob descended on them like hounds. Pierce felt the wind go out of her in a matter of seconds as bodies slammed into her, toppling her over and crushing her into the linoleum floor of the hallway. *Where the fuck had they come from?* Her pistol was knocked from her hand and went clattering down the hall. She felt every footstep as it trudged over her body, kicking her in the face and crunching her ribcage. Then she felt something fall on her—a person?

As she tried to place the sensation, she felt two huge hands close around her windpipe. Amid the chaos, one of the mob must have recognized her. He straddled her midsection, enormous forearms flexing with veins and muscle. Pierce felt her eyes bulge, veins surely popping in her face as she strained to draw breath. As she watched helplessly, the crowd seemed to part around him, allowing him this one kill.

She couldn't believe that this brood of animals—*that Nick fucking Fischer*—would be the reason she died here.

Just as her vision started to turn black, the man's eye exploded, spraying her with something sticky. His hands dropped and he fell sideways off of her and under the feet of the crowd rushing in.

Pierce took huge gulps of air, spots appeared in her vision as she heard a spray of bullets coming from somewhere to her left. There was a rough hand on her shoulder, tugging her up.

"Let's go!" Tom shouted above the crowd. His machine gun was firing wildly into the crowd, people dropping left and right, many backing up as they made their way forward.

"This is our chance," he said. "Get back to the van. Now!"

Pierce barely heard him, but had enough sense to run.

Her vision was spotty, but the scene outside the stadium was chaos. People charged through the doors she'd just come out of. It was clear her orders to run the crowd over hadn't gone well with the civilians outside. As she stumbled into the van they'd left here just minutes ago, a woman came at her screaming, trying to rip Pierce out of the car.

Pierce wound up and kicked the woman in the mouth, hearing the crunch of her teeth breaking. The woman fell and did not get up.

She felt the van rock as Tom leapt into the driver's seat, face bloody but otherwise looking fine. He jammed the key into the ignition and stomped on the gas, hitting a few straggling pedestrians as they peeled out of the parking lot.

"You good, Boss?" he asked.

"Fine," Pierce answered. She looked at the clock. 5:34. They'd missed their ship.

They were stuck here.

Looking at Tom, she saw that he'd registered this as well.

As they turned onto the main drag of downtown, she saw a white Nissan speed by them. She smiled.

"Follow it," she said.

Now

Rory

THEIR FIRST DAY IN THE DARK TOGETHER had passed without incident, and Rory felt thankful. It didn't matter that this happened once a month, she always lost even more sleep during the new moon. It was the one time of the month they had to be totally silent. They sat in the full darkness not making a sound, killing time in the crushing silence. Rory and Sarah had come up with a few silent games to entertain themselves over the years, but today, they have a deck of cards. Between games, they quietly snack on the meager food that's left. They'd have to hunt after this, no doubt about it. Hopefully they'd come across the remains of another town soon—it wasn't ever much, and it was always dangerous, but it allowed them to pick over what was left of the decimated stores.

On the second day, Rory can finally breathe a sigh of relief. *Only a few hours left,* she thinks to herself.

She feels Sarah nudge her. "I need to pee," her daughter whispers.

Damn.

During the new moon, they limited their water intake significantly for this reason. Noise was dangerous, yes. Stepping outside of the tent even more so. The crits were at their most active during these two days, their eyesight totally unblemished. Outside the tent, any movement could easily be seen.

"I need to pee," Sarah says again.

"Okay."

Moving as quietly as possible, they both stand. Rory gently picks up her rifle and unzips the tent. During the new moon, she always goes with Sarah if she has to leave the tent, and simply turns her back to keep watch. They walk less than ten feet from the tent. Sarah squats and Rory turns around to give her some privacy.

There are more stars tonight than she thinks she's ever seen in her life. They span across the sky so bright and unreachable, as though they're looking down, helplessly watching what's left here on Earth. On nights like this, she always thinks of Matt. Is he up there somewhere? Or is that just a bunch of bullshit?

The silence brings her back to reality. Why can't she hear anything yet? She scratches her foot gently against the earth. *Hurry up.*

Silence answers her. Something is wrong.

She turns around slowly, quietly.

Her daughter stands frozen, hands on the zipper of her pants, staring at something. Rory follows her gaze, but Sarah's eyes are so much better, Rory can't see anything but darkness.

It's when she takes a silent step forward that she sees it. A huge shape moving in the darkness, getting closer.

Her blood turns to ice.

At roughly twelve feet tall, the crits are enormous. Six arachnid-like legs make them fast and repulsive. Their skin is slick and leathery, with patches of coarse, black fur stretched tightly across their black bodies, making them look more dead than alive. Rory had seen their jaws full of razor-sharp teeth tear a person apart in seconds. But it was always the eyes for her. Two bulging, black orbs in the middle of that dead face. Smooth enough to look as though they were made of glass, sharp enough to see everything.

Her knees threaten to buckle. If she'd gasped, she'd have given them away and it would have ended right then. The rifle on her shoulder feels heavy, reminding her it's there. She lifts it, one silent centimeter at a time.

The crit draws closer, closer, closer. It hasn't seen them yet.

The gun is on her shoulder now. How much time has passed? She can't tell. An eternity. Her finger moves to turn the safety off. Why hadn't she done that before leaving the tent?

The crit is fifteen yards away. How has it not seen them?

Rory finds the safety.

Click.

The crit's head whips around. Its huge, black eyes glued on them now. It *hisses,* and lurches forward at a full sprint, directly at them.

Shit, Rory thinks. *This is it.*

Time slows. Her finger is on the trigger. It is their only hope, but it will likely prove useless and the discharge will only bring an army of crits to the tent. *Fucking* new moon. She watches her daughter take one staggering step backwards. In a flash, Rory remembers Sarah's whole life—the day she was born, Matt rocking her to sleep, her first steps, their journey together through the darkness.

Take care of our daughter, he'd said.

She aims the rifle.

The crit comes to a screeching halt. It's eyes full of hatred. *Is it scared of the gun?* She thinks.

Then out of the corner of her eye, she sees a small shape appear next to her.

Rory looks down to her left. Jacob has emerged silently from the tent and stands next to her now. All she can see are his huge eyes and one of his arms raised, extending an open palm toward the crit.

Rory yanks her eyes from Jacob and looks back at the crit in awe—it's shaking, but otherwise frozen. She realizes its hateful stare isn't aimed at her, but at Jacob. Its black eyes are in agony, its teeth bared. It makes a whimpering sound Rory has never heard before.

"No," Jacob whispers, the puff of his breath making a tiny steam cloud in the air. He raises his other hand. Both palms are open now, extended out towards the crit. It takes one shaking step backwards.

What the—

The next movement is so slight Rory would have missed it if she hadn't been standing right next to the boy. Jacob exhales, breath swirling out around him like cigarette smoke, and *pushes.*

The crit slides backward, its knees buckling underneath it. It stumbles and falls as its tarantula legs flail out, looking for purchase.

Rory can't breathe. Her eyes flick back and forth between Jacob and the crit.

Jacob, arms still out, takes a step forward. The crit whimpers again, scrambling to get away.

"No," he repeats.

The crit slides back another few feet until, finally, it finds a foothold and picks itself up. It stumbles and falls, crumpling in pain as it backs away. When it stands, it turns and crawls back to the forest beyond. They hear its footsteps *retreat, retreat, retreat,* until finally, the silence returns—and with it, a sliver of moonlight.

Sarah turns and lets out a shaking breath. Her right pant leg is soaked. Rory looks down at Jacob, who stares after the crit, arms back down at his sides. Sam has emerged from the tent behind them, and Rory looks up at him, mouth hanging open and eyes huge.

"We should talk," he whispers.

2074-2075

Then

SAM

DRIVING A CAR WASN'T AN OPTION when they set out from Jacksonville. The streets were too crowded with abandoned, destroyed cars from The Collapse.

So they walked.

"Jesus, it's freezing, eh?" Chet said, rubbing his gloved hands together.

"I thought your generation was all about global warming," Sam smiled. "What happened to that?"

"*That* was your entire life before now," Chet laughed. "That's what got us here, buddy."

"Right about now, I'd take that over this," Becca said, pulling her coat more tightly around her as they trudged through the littered streets.

The Main Street Bridge was nearly impassable. Several of the abandoned cars had sustained damage from the mass exodus during The Collapse, front ends smashed in like accordions and windows shattered. Some, they could see, had nose-dived off the bridge entirely, breaking through the protective barriers and plummeting into the river below. There were bodies everywhere. Some looked much newer than others. Some with obvious bullet holes, some that had clearly been torn to shreds by crits. Sam didn't look too closely. Becca did.

"Come on, Bec," Sam said, when she'd stopped to stare down at something.

She didn't answer.

Sam looked over at Chet, who shrugged. They walked over to her.

As Sam approached, he began to see what his wife was looking at. In front of her was the partially decomposed body of a woman, holding a small, frozen bundle in her arms.

Sam turned and vomited when he realized it was their old neighbor, still holding tight to her baby daughter.

"God help us," Chet said under his breath.

"I remember the day she told me they were leaving," Becca said. "They didn't have a car, so they were gonna try and make it on foot," her voice broke. "Jesus," she said, shaking. "They didn't even make it outside the city."

Chet reached down and gently tugged free the baby blanket still clutched in the woman's hand. With unbelievable care, he draped it over the mother and daughter. "Now they don't have to see any more of this world," he said quietly, wiping a tear from his eye.

Sam wiped his mouth and tried to collect himself. He pulled his hat farther down his head and looked around, out over the bridge, trying to make sense of what had once been downtown Jacksonville. As he surveyed the total silence and the miles of destruction, he realized it would never make sense. He took a deep breath and took Becca's hand.

"Come on," he said. "We've got a long way to go."

Eventually they cleared the city limits and headed west,

avoiding major highways and relying on the few maps they'd gathered up before departing. They passed the time telling stories—mostly Chet, who Sam found he loved more and more each day. Mostly because his stories kept their minds on something other than what was left of America.

"I grew up with three older brothers," he told them one day. "My mother was a saint, and my father was the most even-keeled person you ever met. I remember we were driving down our street in Madison one day after it had just snowed—one of the last times that ever happened. My parents were in the front seats and my brothers and I were all crammed in the back. One of the neighborhood kids threw a snowball right through one of the back windows and into the car. It exploded on the rearview mirror."

Sam chuckled, imagining it.

"You know what my dad did? Nothing. Just reached up, wiped off the mirror, and kept driving." Chet laughed. "Unflappable, that guy was."

"Can I ask what happened to your brothers?" Becca said.

"One got deployed to Russia back in '35 and never came home," Chet said. "The other two lived long, happy lives and passed a few years ago. Terrible melanoma. They were both about ten years older than me—the unplanned one."

As they walked, they learned about what Chet's life had been like, how his job in construction had kept him active his whole life, and the tragedy of his wife's illness that, eventually, brought him to Florida.

"And what about you two?" Chet asked them. "How did you meet?"

Becca smiled. She loved this story.

"Go on," Sam said to her. "You tell it better than I do."

"Okay," she laughed. "I was living in Phoenix at the time, working in advertising—a few years before we shut down for good. He was in Jacksonville already, teaching. My friend was getting married to his friend, and I texted her before the wedding to ask if there were any cute guys going. She sent me his picture, I thought he was cute, and she sat us next to each other at the reception."

"Now *that's* what I call a good friend!" Chet said.

"That's what I thought," Becca said, laughing. "Anyway, we hit it off and…the rest is history."

Chet sighed. "What's the saying? 'I wish we knew it when we were in the good old days'?"

. . .

The days were long. Sam's lower back throbbed every day for the first few weeks. Becca's feet blistered and Chet's arthritic knees ached so badly that they had to stop frequently, resting for several days at a time in abandoned homes when they could. It would be slow going to Calgary, but at least it was something to do—a goal to look forward to instead of wasting away in their apartment building. Once their bodies began to adjust to the mileage every day, they started to go farther and farther.

But they could always hear the screams at night. The crits were never far from their minds, though they had yet to see any out on the road.

They stayed off the beaten path as much as possible, taking back roads they found on their maps and steering clear of major cities. Somewhere just west of Oklahoma City, they stumbled into a small town called Elk City. It looked like something out of an old western, like it had been abandoned long before The Collapse.

At the outskirts of town, they spotted what looked like a deserted house in the middle of an open field. It was a two-story mammoth of a home with a wrap-around porch that still sported several benches. Acres of flat, gray farmland stretched out around it. This house had been loved, once.

"Must've been a real beaut back in the sunlight," Chet said. "We should check it out."

They'd taken to scoping out abandoned houses in search of supplies. So far, they'd mostly hit homes that had obviously been pillaged by others passing through, but they always managed to find some useful leftovers. You never know what you might need on the road.

"It's too dangerous," said Becca. "I don't like it here. Something's not right."

"I agree," Chet said. "But if they have any supplies in there, we all know it's worth the risk."

"Sam?" Becca said.

He looked at both of them and sighed. "I'm sorry, Bec," he said. "I'm with Chet on this."

She pursed her lips.

"You stay here for now," Sam started, "Chet and I will—"

"Like hell," Becca said, starting off toward the house.

Chet tried to hide his smile.

As they got closer, they slowed their pace, ducking down behind some scant bushes in the field in front of the house. They were hoping to see if anyone was inside.

"I don't see anything," Chet said. "Let's go."

Slowly, silently, they crept toward the house

Chet approached first, checking the front door to see if

it was locked. It wasn't, as was usually the case. He eased it open and stepped across the threshold, his rifle raised and ready. But he fired no shots. Instead, he waved his hand to summon them.

Coast is clear.

Sam and Becca followed close behind.

They entered the house into a kitchen that looked like it had once, long ago, been filled with love. There were floral placemats still on the table and children's drawings on the refrigerator. Chet was probably right—the picture window in the kitchen would've given whoever lived here a beautiful view, back in the sunlight.

Most of the shelves had been picked over, but there were still a few gems available: soups, canned fruit, and—miraculously—running water.

"They must have a well that's still active," Chet said smiling. "You guys grab what you can in here, I'll check the bathroom for meds."

Sam turned and began loading whatever food he could find into his bag. He was amazed by the running water and couldn't help smiling as he filled up their bottles. *What a life of luxury we lived before this,* he thought.

Then he heard a door open down the hall. Something crashed.

"Whoa whoa whoa, easy!" Chet yelled.

Sam's heart stopped. But he had enough training to know, immediately, to stay calm. He instinctively crossed the room to Becca, just as Chet and a young man entered the kitchen.

"Easy, kid, easy," said Chet. He was slowly backing away from the door, hands raised.

The stranger was tall and scrawny with dark hair that fell

over his eyes in a curtain. He looked like he hadn't had a decent meal maybe ever. He was young, early twenties at most.

"What the fuck are you doing in here?" the kid asked.

Sam's heart was racing, but he kept his breathing even. "We thought this place was abandoned," he said calmly, hands raised. "We see now that it's not. We'll just go, okay?"

The kid turned the gun toward Sam and Becca. Without missing a beat, Chet moved to stand directly in front of it.

"Hey," Chet said. "There's no need for any of this. Like my friend said, we're leaving, okay?"

Just then, another man walked into the house, saw them, and froze.

"What the fuck, Benny?" the new guy said to the kid, moving into the room. "We can't leave you here alone for one fucking hour?"

We? Sam thought. He grabbed Becca's hand, squeezed it.

"I didn't even hear them come in!" Benny shouted back. "Plus, I got 'em now," he said, raising the gun once again at Chet.

"Look, we'll just leave," Becca said. "We'll put everything back and—"

"Shut up," said the new guy. He looked at his partner. "We need to deal with this before they all get back."

He grabbed a pistol from the holster on his hip and aimed it at Chet.

"No!" Sam shouted. But as the word came out, he realized he wasn't the only one who'd said it. A little boy with bright eyes had appeared at the door. He was barely visible under so many layers of clothing, but he held his arms out straight with his palms open, pointing directly at the two men who now stared back at him, frozen.

Sam never forgot how strange they looked. How terrified

and confused. It was like they were straining against themselves. One tried to speak but couldn't.

"No," the boy spoke again, quietly. Then, very gently, he pushed.

The two men were lifted into the air and blasted back through the enormous dining room window. In a spray of blood and glass, they landed on the frozen ground outside with a *thud*. Neither of them moved.

Sam, Becca, and Chet stood in stunned silence, staring at the boy, who lowered his arms and stared back.

"How did you—" Becca started, but Chet cut her off, gaining control of his shock first.

"We need to leave," he said. "They said there's more coming."

Becca nodded.

Quickly, Sam gathered up the supplies, scavenging the drawers and cupboards for more, and shoved them in a bag.

Becca approached the boy.

"Where are your parents?" she asked.

The boy shrugged.

"Are they close by somewhere?" she said.

The boy shook his head no.

"Are you with anyone? A group, or someone taking care of you?"

He shook his head again.

Becca looked up at Sam, who nodded.

"I know you don't know us," she said gently. "But if you want to come with us, it's safe. We won't hurt you."

The boy nodded.

"Okay," she said. "What's your name, honey?"

The boy stared at her, then, so quietly they could barely hear, he said, "Jacob."

2076

Now

Rory

Rory and Sarah stare at Sam in disbelief, trying to digest what he's just told them.

"But how can he—" Rory starts.

"I don't know," Sam says. "He just can."

They stare at Jacob, who's nestled himself back against Sam. He looks so *ordinary*. Like any other little kid in the world. But what he'd done out there with his *bare hands…*

"When he told us that he wasn't with anyone—no friends, no family, all three of us sort of stepped into that role as well as we could, until…" he breaks off, looking down. "Well, now it's just me."

Rory is still somewhere between fear, shock, and appreciation, but she can't help feeling heartbroken for Sam, too. She knows the pain of losing your life partner and your closest friends all too well.

"Anyway, we all knew we had to take care of him. He can just…*do* things. Things other people can't do. If the wrong people found him…"

"They would try and use him," Rory finishes solemnly.

"Exactly," Sam says. "They'd think he was the answer or

something. And maybe he is, I don't know. But I'm not forcing him into anything. He's just a kid."

"How old *are* you?" Sarah asks Jacob bluntly, who retreats further into Sam.

"He doesn't say much," Sam says. "But from what I've gotten out of him, I think he's about ten."

"Wow," Sarah says. Then she smiles, "that's pretty bad ass, you know," she says to Jacob, who smiles shyly. "Thank you for what you did out there."

"You saved us," Rory says, reaching out tentatively to squeeze his shoulder. "Thank you."

Jacob smiles.

"So" Sarah continues, looking at Sam. The matter of them traveling with a telekinetic child apparently settled. "You guys heard the broadcast? When?"

"Shortly after they aired it," Sam says. "It took us a long time to decide to follow it. Chet convinced us, in the end."

Sarah and Rory nod, understanding. It had taken them a long time as well.

Sam looks at Sarah. "Even if the broadcast is real, if this place in Canada is really there, it'll be dangerous," his eyes flick to Rory's for a moment, then back to Sarah. "I'm going to teach you a few things before we get there," he says.

Sarah's face lights up, her smile huge. "I heard," she replies.

Sam smiles sadly. "You may have heard," he says, "but you don't understand."

"Understand what?" Sarah asks.

Sam and Rory exchange a look.

"What you might need to do to survive in this world," Sam answers.

Sarah looks at her quickly. Rory nods her head once.

"We start tomorrow," Sam finishes.

That night, Rory dreams of Jacob.

2074

Then

Jacob

"Jacob, get up," Paul whispered.

He was still groggy, wondering why Paul was shaking him in the middle of the night. Then he remembered he'd slept at Paul's house while his parents said they were doing something for work that night.

"What's going on?" Jacob replied.

He heard a scream outside the window and was immediately afraid. Paul's eyes were huge, so Jacob knew his friend was, too.

"We have to go right now," Paul said, yanking him out of bed.

Jacob's eyes welled with tears. "What's happening?" he asked.

Paul forced a smile, and Jacob remembered that even though he seemed like an older brother, Paul was still just a kid, too. "It's gonna be okay," Paul said. "But we need to hurry."

The two boys rushed down the stairs to find Paul's parents, fully dressed in the middle of the night, sun shining through the blackout curtains. Another scream came from outside. Jacob froze.

"Where are my parents?" he asked. He was so confused.

"We're going to them right now," Paul's mom said. "Are you guys ready?"

"Ready for what?" Jacob asked. "What's going on?"

"I'm sorry sweetie," Paul's mom answered. "We'll explain everything soon."

"We need to move," said Paul's dad.

Paul reached down to grab Jacob's hand. "Don't worry buddy," he said. "It's gonna be okay."

Paul's parents led them out the door and into the car. As the car moved through the streets, Jacob noticed things were mostly quiet, since most people were asleep. But something wasn't right. Jacob knew it.

The further they drove, the colder Jacob started to feel, even though they hadn't been driving more than ten minutes. He recognized where they were headed—this was the way to his mom's office.

As they pulled into the parking lot and approached the building, Jacob could see why his mom had stopped bringing him here over a year ago. The darkness had consumed a portion of the office, cutting across in a clean, black line. He'd only ever seen the darkness from a distance—this was the closest he'd ever been.

"My God," Paul's dad said. "I didn't realize how bad it was."

"Mom, are you sure we should be doing this?" Paul asked.

"We don't have another option, honey," she replied. "The darkness is coming too fast, and—"

Her sentence was cut off. A woman careened out from the darkness and sprinted past their car screaming, blood pumping from the stump that was once her arm.

Paul screamed.

"Are my parents in there?" Jacob yelled.

Paul's parents exchanged a look in the front seat. Jacob knew what it meant.

"We can't go in there. Not anymore," Paul's dad said. "They said the darkness hadn't even reached it yesterday."

"What?" his mom answered. "What other choice do we have?"

"Are my parents in there!" Jacob yelled this time.

"They are, but sweetie—" Paul's mom started, but Jacob had heard enough. He jumped out of the car and ran full speed into the building.

. . .

"MOM!" Jacob screamed as the door slammed behind him. "Dad! Where are you?"

He spun around, trying to remember where he was in the enormous building and how to get to his mom's office.

He noticed how cold it was. Freezing, actually. As he stared down the long hallway, he realized the only light source came from the ones hanging above his head. Outside the windows, it was total darkness. He started to shake.

"Mom," he whispered, "where are you?"

As he rounded a corner, he heard a scuffling noise from down the hall. He strained his ears, trying to place it. There was a chittering noise—something he'd never heard before.

"Mom?"

An enormous, black spidery creature rounded the corner straight ahead of him. Its black eyes bore into him, teeth gnashing.

Jacob had never felt fear like he did then. His stomach

dropped like a rock inside him. The monster was more than twice his father's height with legs that made his skin crawl. It looked at him with pure hatred, and something else. Hunger. Was this the thing his teachers had been training him for? Before he could consider the question, the monster charged. He was so terrified he couldn't even scream. He knew he would be dead in seconds.

It was ten feet away, then five, then one. It was so close that when it opened its mouth, Jacob could see bits of flesh hanging from its rows of razor-sharp teeth. He closed his eyes, and then…nothing.

When he opened them, the monster was lying in a heap against the far wall. He didn't understand.

"Jacob!" someone said behind him.

He turned to see Paul and his parents standing there, arms outstretched toward the monster. His friend looked as scared and shocked as Jacob felt.

"Come on," Paul said, lowering his arm to reach for Jacob's hand. "Let's go."

The four of them raced through the hallways of the building, going further and further into the dark. With every step, it got colder. He wanted to ask where they were going, what that thing back there was, but he was so scared he could barely move, let alone speak.

"You're sure it was this way?" Paul's dad said up ahead.

"I'm sure," his mom answered.

Around every corner, Jacob was sure another monster would appear. But the whole time, Paul stayed right with him holding his hand as they ran.

"It's gonna be okay," Paul said. "We're almost there."

Finally, they passed through another set of doors Jacob had never seen, and on the other side were his parents.

"Mom!" he shouted, collapsing into her arms.

"Oh, thank god," she whispered over and over. "Thank God."

He looked around. There were so many people here. He saw a bunch of his classmates and wondered what everyone was doing here in the middle of the night. "What's going on?" he asked.

His mom squeezed him tight. "Thank you so much," she said to Paul's parents. "Gabe is over there getting—"

A horrible screeching sound pierced the room. All the parents turned toward the noise. That's when Jacob heard the chittering again. All the hair on the back of his neck stood up. There was more than one, even he could tell.

"Get the kids on the ships!" Gabe, his mom's boss yelled.

"Mom?" Paul said, turning to his mother. "What does he—?"

"There's no time," Paul's mom said. "Go with Jacob and his mom. I love you." She hugged him fiercely and ran toward the sound of the monsters.

Jacob felt his mom grab his and Paul's hands before she took off in the opposite direction, just as the doors behind them blasted open. A dozen monsters barrelled through.

"MOM!" Paul screamed.

Behind them, Jacob saw a monster go flying. He tried to crane his neck, but his mom's grip was iron-tight on his wrist.

"Come on!" his mother screamed.

They ran outside into the pitch darkness. Jacob's heart threatened to beat through his chest.

"Get to the ship ahead!" his mom ordered. "Stay together!"

Jacob could see tears streaming down Paul's face as he once again reached for Jacob's hand. "Come on," Paul said.

Just ahead, Jacob could make out a row of metal tubes.

These must be the ships. Over the last few months, he'd heard his parents talking about them when they thought he couldn't hear.

There was a man waiting outside a ship up ahead, waving them in. "Come on!" he shouted.

"But what about—" Jacob started.

"Get in!"

Jacob's entire body was shaking. He and Paul ducked into the ship, which looked like a big cylinder lined with rows of chairs and seatbelts. Paul threw Jacob into one of the seats in the back, buckling him in before taking the seat right next to him.

"It's gonna be okay," Paul said. "We're safe."

An explosion thundered behind them, lighting up the world around them for a split second. In the flash of light, Jacob saw the chaos all around them. People ran in every direction, trying to get on a ship or fight off the monsters.

Jacob had a moment to wonder where his mom was before the blast jolted their ship sideways. He cracked his head hard against the wall.

Everything went black.

2076

Now

Sarah

She'd waited years to be around people again. *Good* people. She'd been pretty young during The Collapse, but she remembered what the people had been like. At first, they just gave her the creeps. But then, as things got crazier, they actually scared the shit out of her. Her parents had pulled her out of school, she could barely leave the house without supervision, and anyone outside of friends or family was totally off-limits. But she'd missed people desperately—and she hadn't even realized it until meeting Sam and Jacob.

"Okay," Sam says. "Quick, basic defensive maneuvers will be first."

It's their first day of training. They've been walking all day and she is exhausted, but Sam says that's a good thing.

"You need to be ready to fight at any moment—especially when you're tired."

Sarah thought that had sounded really badass when he'd said it this morning, but now she's hungry and spent. They've been perfecting her punch for the last thirty minutes. Her hand is preemptively wrapped in a cloth bandage, but she knows it will still be bruised as she punches it over

87

and over again into their makeshift bag—a couple of sleeping bags against a backpack that Sam is holding, which muffles most of the sound of each punch.

"Again," Sam says as she throws all of her strength into a right hook. "The key to any good hit—punch, elbow, whatever—is to put all your weight behind it."

He holds up his hand for her to stop and gives her the sleeping bags.

"All of your energy comes up from the ground," he says, taking a stagger-step stance to demonstrate. "Twist your hips, and use that momentum to hit," on the last word, his fist lands with such force she nearly stumbles backwards. "Now you try."

Sarah plants her feet firmly in the same stance she'd just watched Sam take. She looks at the sleeping bags, musters up all her rage, turns her hips, and brings her fist around to swing through the backpack. The blow is so hard that she fears for a moment she'd ripped through one of the sleeping bags.

Sam lowers the bag. "Good," he smiles. "Very good. Now let's work on dodging a hit from an opponent."

They spend the rest of the hour working on speed during a fight—dodging blows, footwork, and reaction times. She can see her mother watching out of the corner of her eye and wonders how things might've gone that night at the lake if she'd had this training. She puts the thought out of her head. It doesn't matter. They'd gotten away then, and next time she'll be ready.

Because if she'd learned anything living this life in the darkness, it's that sooner or later, there's a next time.

2076

Now

Rory

The broadcast had apparently aired a few months after The Collapse, but Rory had only heard it about six months back when she found a small, battery-operated radio in a drugstore somewhere outside of El Paso. For a long time, there was only static. But for whatever reason, Rory had kept tuning in. It felt good to do *something* to feel connected to the outside world. And then one night, like a dream, the static crackled to life.

"If there's anyone out there who can hear me, my name is Gabe. Today is June 15th...calling from Calgary...leftover ships....security here in large numbers...safety...."

The message played over and over across the otherwise empty airwaves, and eventually they'd pieced it together. There was a place in Calgary where some of the colonization ships had never left. It was safe, there was security, there was a community there trying to save as many as they could.

Or so they said.

She had agonized over the decision. They'd been traveling south for so long, the thought of turning around and going north was nearly unbearable. And was it even true? She couldn't shake the thought of the last encounter they'd had with a man in this new world. If there had been more….

The thought was too horrible.

But hope, as always with human nature, had outweighed her fears. She had a daughter to think of. She would never let anyone hurt Sarah. And if there was a hope for a real life—even just a sliver—they had to take it. So they'd turned around, abandoning the thought of warmer weather, and made their way back north.

For better or worse.

. . .

Rory has to admit that the last week has been better with Sam and Jacob. Since the new moon ended, allowing them to talk quietly together, Sam and Sarah haven't been able to shut up. It's a beautiful thing to watch. Sarah has always been strong; she's always done what's expected of her and has rarely complained. But around Sam, she's filled with a light Rory has never seen. They talk all day and train at night. Sam's fighting skills hold up—he's taught Sarah far better than anything Rory had ever been able to teach her. Sam was right, they do need each other.

Just as Sarah is drawn to Sam, Jacob seems drawn to Rory. The small boy still never utters a word, but he walks alongside Rory all day, keeping a surprisingly fast pace for such a small kid. Although he doesn't talk back, Rory often talks to him during the day, and she's seen him smile more than once. She wants to know so much about him, but she has to be patient. He'll talk when he's ready.

"So have you always been able to stop the crits like you did the other night?" Rory asks him one day.

Nothing. Just the *pat pat pat* of his little feet on the frozen ground.

"Are you afraid of them?"

Pat pat pat.

"It's okay if you are, you know. I am."

Pat pat pat.

Rory looks down, nods. Satisfied with the silence.

"Me too," says that little voice.

The sound is so shocking that Rory almost trips over her own feet. She looks down at Jacob, willing him to say more. But he doesn't. That's all for now. So Rory nods.

"Well, that's okay. The only time you can be brave is when you're afraid," Rory says. She'd read that somewhere a million years ago, in another life.

"I miss them," Jacob says.

Rory's heart palpitates.

"Who?" she asks, trying to sound casual.

"Everyone," he says.

She stops to look at him, "Who is everyone, Jacob?"

He looks up at her with those bright green eyes, and she realizes she's pushed too hard, too soon. He shrugs, turns away from her, and keeps walking.

She kicks herself and follows.

2075

Then

Sam

They were all fascinated by Jacob, who'd barely uttered a word in the weeks since he'd saved them. He was young— Sam guessed about eight or nine. *How* had he done that? A few nights ago at their campfire, Jacob had made a water bottle levitate toward him when he was thirsty. They'd all sat there, staring and dumbfounded as Jacob sipped the water in silence.

"You know," Chet had whispered, "it's pretty cool you can do that. I don't think any of us can, right guys?" he gestured to Sam and Becca, who shook their heads. "How did you learn to move things without touching them?"

They looked at Jacob, each of them holding their breath.

He just shrugged.

Sam had so many questions, but it was clear they wouldn't get much from Jacob. He couldn't blame the kid. Who knew what the hell he'd been through? Sam and Becca's musings ranged from radioactive poisoning to a top-secret government weapon. But really, they had no idea.

Chet, who had lost his own son to a childhood illness brought on by excessive sun exposure, was particularly taken with Jacob. The two of them walked together all day, Becca

92

and Sam trailing behind as Chet waved his arms, making Jacob laugh.

"What do you think they talk about?" Becca asked.

"I think Chet is doing most of the talking," Sam chuckled. He lowered his voice. "Does having him here, Jacob I mean, ever make you regret…"

"Not having kids?" Becca asked, raising an eyebrow. "No way," she continued, gesturing around to the dark, frozen landscape. "Look around. That poor kid will never know normalcy. He'll spend his entire life in this." She took his hand and squeezed it. "We made the right call."

. . .

"I hope you like canned beans," Chet said that night at their campfire, pouring Jacob's dinner into a bowl. "We haven't seen much game lately, but I think we'll have some better options when we get into Utah."

After the abandoned house a few weeks back, they'd decided to keep heading west, turn north in Arizona, and head toward Utah. Just in case whoever Jacob had thrown through those windows had heard the broadcast and felt like following them. The desert terrain had been terrible for hunting, and on top of it, the darkness had killed off millions of animals. Sure, they had more hope for Utah, but they had much further to go until they truly left the desert.

"I know these are kind of slimy," Chet went on, totally unfazed by Jacob's lack of response. "But you know what's fun about them? They make you—" Chet stuck out his tongue and made a farting sound. Jacob's eyes grew huge with delight and he actually giggled.

"Just ask Becca," Chet continued. "Hers are the worst of all of us!"

Becca gasped, then snorted a laugh. "Hey!" she said. "That is *not* true. Don't believe him Jacob. He farts without needing any beans."

Sam and Jacob both laughed, and Sam couldn't help beaming at his wife. He couldn't remember the last time he'd seen her like this.

"Well she's got me there," Chet went on. "So, Jacob, what did you use to eat with your family?"

Jacob, predictable as always, just shrugged.

"When I was a kid," Chet went on, "my favorite meal was always at Thanksgiving. It's a day when you celebrate with everyone you love and eat a big, fat turkey. Do you like turkey?"

Jacob shrugged. "Not sure," he said quietly.

Becca and Sam looked at each other—*had Jacob spoken?* Chet looked up and winked at them.

"Well, we'll have to change that," Chet said. "One day we'll have a nice, big turkey together," he said. "How does that sound?"

"Sounds good," Jacob said, smiling.

. . .

"The trick with kids," Chet said to Sam the next day, "is to just keep talking and asking them questions. Sooner or later, they'll respond. Whatever this kid's story is, can you even imagine what he's seen out here? Who knows how long he's been alone? Of course he doesn't want to talk."

Sam nodded. Jacob was so young—he couldn't imagine the kind of trauma he'd been through. Though Jacob barely spoke, he'd started to open a soft spot in them all. They all knew they had to try and give him the best life they could in this dying world—which meant making it to Canada. It was likely the kid had been to hell and back, and still, he'd saved them all. Now they had to return the favor.

They'd just reached Sedona and were looking for a place to camp when they heard the rumbling of an engine behind them. Sam's heart jumped into his throat. They'd thought about trying to find a vehicle, but ever since they'd made a run for it at that abandoned house, they hadn't found anything viable.

Sam turned and saw headlights bearing down on them from behind. They'd been seen.

2074

Then

JACOB

HE UNBUCKLED HIS SEATBELT AND LOOKED AROUND, DAZED. His head hurt so much and there was glass everywhere. He remembered nothing but the monsters. Slowly, he crawled through the debris inside the ship to find his mom.

He found her in the front of the ship, slouched down at a strange angle. Her eyes were closed.

"Mom," he whispered. "Wake up."

She didn't move.

Jacob figured she must be asleep and started to make his way out into the darkness, where he could hear voices.

"Oh, Jacob, you're okay!" Someone shouted to him. When he looked up, realized it was Paul. "Did anyone else wake up?"

"No," Jacob said. "What's going on?"

"Come here," Paul says, guiding him out of the ship and onto the grass. "What do you remember?"

"Not much."

"Okay," Paul says. "We had to leave really fast…there was an explosion when we were leaving, do you remember that? You hit your head really hard, and I think it knocked you out."

That explains that.

"Your mom…"

"She made it back to the ship," Jacob said. "She's just sleeping," he points back to where he'd seen her.

Paul looked down.

"What?" Jacob asked.

"We didn't…the ship crashed, Jacob," Paul said. "She made it back that night, but…I'm so sorry. Your mom is gone."

"What do you mean? She's right there."

And then it hit him.

He ran back to the ship and crawled to his mother. He noticed her lips had started to turn blue. He reached out to touch her hand. It was cold. Her calm breathing, that he only now noticed had been a steady presence in his life, had stopped. His whole body started to shake. He turned to look at Paul. He didn't realize he was crying until he could barely see his friend's face.

"I'm so sorry, Jacob," Paul said. "But we have to keep going. You said you remember the monsters, right? They're here, too."

2076

Now

SARAH

A FEW WEEKS HAVE PASSED WITH THEIR NEW COMPANIONS, and Sarah and her mom have already learned a lot about them.

Now, Sarah stands facing Sam again as they work through their nightly training session. In just a few weeks, she already feels stronger and faster. Not only are they practicing fighting techniques, but she's building her strength. She does pushups, sit-ups, and even pull-ups whenever they can find a decaying tree branch strong enough to hold her weight.

"You need to be strong if someone attacks you from any angle," Sam says. "But particularly from behind. They'll likely try and pin your arms to your sides so you can't move. But the stronger you get, the better chance you have of preventing that or freeing yourself.

"If someone gets your arms pinned," he went on, "you try to push your elbows out and away from your body, and drive down with your fist into their groin as hard as you can, then sidestep and run."

She nods.

"Let's practice the motion a few times." They practice it over and over. They practice driving the heel of her palm into someone's nose. They do more pushups. More sit-ups. More pull-ups.

"You don't always have to be stronger than your opponent to win," Sam says. "A lot of times, just putting up a fight is enough. If they know you won't be an easy target, most people will quit.

"Remember," he says, eyes locking on hers. "Your attacker is going to be a coward. They want someone weak so it's an easy win. We're not going to give them that."

Sarah nods. She had been an easy target once. She would never be again.

No one could ever take the place of her father, but Sam is slowly stepping into the role as much as he can, she realizes, for her and for Jacob.

She plants her feet, turns her hips, and drives her palm upward against the backpack Sam is holding, practicing how she could break someone's nose in a frontal attack.

"Good," Sam says. "Again."

2075

Then

SAM

"RUN!" CHET YELLED.

Sam grabbed Jacob's hand and took off at a sprint, following Chet and Becca. The desert landscape offered little cover. There was nothing but dying cacti and rocky mountain faces around them. There was nowhere to hide.

The vehicle behind them was getting closer, its rumbling growing louder by the second. *God help us.*

They were bathed in the yellow glare of approaching headlights. A voice spoke over an intercom. "Drop your fucking weapons," a man said. "Or we kill you all right now."

They stopped. Sam's heart hammered in his chest. *How the fuck are we gonna get out of this?* He looked at Jacob, who was frozen in terror, eyes wide, clinging to him.

Chet took a deep breath, "Alright," he said. "Everybody just calm down." He put down his rifle. Becca and Sam did the same. Sam couldn't see anything through those blinding yellow headlights.

"Cuff 'em," the voice said. The headlights went out.

Sam's eyes adjusted in time to see four men jump out of a black Jeep. As they came closer, he saw the two from the abandoned house. *Bastards.* The other two he didn't recognize. They were huge with unruly black hair.

The two from the house approached with zip ties, securing all of their hands behind their backs.

"On their knees," said the one who'd been talking over the loudspeaker.

Sam felt someone kick the back of his knees and he dropped into the rock-hard dirt. Jacob was to his left, then Becca, then Chet.

"We heard y'all had a nice time at our house a few weeks back," the one who'd talked through the loudspeaker—their apparent leader—said through a mouth full of yellow teeth. "Didn't your parents ever teach you not to steal?"

"Just do what you're gonna do," Chet said, words full of venom. "But the boy had nothing to do with it. Let him go, at least."

"From what I hear," Yellow Teeth said. "The boy had *everything* to do with it. So he's first."

From the corner of his eye, Sam saw Jacob startle. He was shaking like a leaf. *Please don't let this be happening,* Sam thought. *Don't let them hurt him.*

"Cowards," Becca spat. "Fucking cowards."

"You know," Yellow Teeth said, looking at Becca. "We might just keep you around for entertainment," Sam's blood boiled. "You'd like that, wouldn't you? What do you think, boys?" The other men laughed, leering at her.

Yellow Teeth raised his pistol at Jacob.

"*No!*" Sam and Chet shouted at once.

But it was Becca who moved—leaning hard to her right, lurching herself awkwardly in front of Jacob. As she moved, there was a chittering noise behind Yellow Teeth. The scurrying of six spider legs.

A gunshot pierced the air as the man whipped around toward the noise. He had time for one word:

"Fuck."

One moment he was there and the next—in a spray of red—he was gone. Sam saw an amputated arm flop to the ground, fingers still twitching. He uselessly tried to crawl for cover, which was impossible with his hands bound behind his back. He sucked up flakes of cold dirt as he tried to inch himself forward like a worm, curling up his knees and kicking them out again. The ground bit into his face. He heard nothing but the screams around him as their attackers tried to outrun the crit.

Suddenly, Sam felt the zip ties snap off his wrists. He looked up to see Jacob standing next to him with a shaking hand raised.

"Thanks, Jacob," he yelled over the noise. "What about the others?" It was difficult to see through the dark mayhem around them.

Jacob didn't answer.

The chaos reached a crescendo. The crit swiped its huge legs left and right, tearing the men apart as they screamed and tried to run for cover.

With his hands free, Sam searched frantically for a weapon—anything to defend them with. There was no question that when the crit finished off their attackers, they were next.

"Becca!" he yelled. "Can you find a weapon?"

He heard Becca groan and turned, finally, to look at her.

There was a small hole squarely in her chest, blood blooming on her shirt faster and faster. In the commotion, he'd thought the gunshot Yellow Teeth fired had gone wide. But it hadn't. It had hit his wife directly in the heart.

"No," Sam breathed. "No, please, no no no."

There was so much blood. It pumped out of her like a faucet, ceaseless, no matter how he tried to cover it. Their captors were screaming, running in all directions to escape the crit. Jacob must have freed Chet, and Sam numbly registered their presence beside him.

"Oh no," Chet whispered, lowering his head.

"Sam…" Becca breathed. Blood bubbled out of her mouth.

He knelt down next to her and held her head in his hands. "Please, baby," he said. "Don't leave."

Chet's hand went to his mouth as tears streamed down his face. "Oh, Becca," he breathed. He put an arm around Jacob.

"Take care of him," Becca said, looking at Jacob.

"Don't talk like that," Sam answered, eyes streaming.

"You…need to go," she whispered. "Now."

"No, you're gonna be okay," Sam said. "I just need…Chet, help me!"

"Sam," Chet said firmly, sadness etched into every line of his kind face, "We have to get out of here." Though his voice broke on the last word, he put a hand on Sam, who smacked it away.

"Don't fucking touch me," Sam said. He could barely see as he turned to his dying wife. "You're gonna be okay," he whispered again.

Becca smiled. "I love you," she said. And then, as if going to sleep, she sighed and shut her eyes.

"Oh God," Sam said, his voice breaking. "Somebody help me. Chet, please, help me!"

As if in some strange chorus, Sam heard the screams of one of their captors behind him, mingling with his own. The man's gun discharged again and again, his final stand against the crit, a stand they all knew wouldn't be enough.

Sam cradled his wife's lifeless body in his arms, rocking her back and forth. He didn't care what happened. Not now. She couldn't be gone. This couldn't be real.

"Sam!" Chet said, grabbing Sam's shoulders this time and shaking him. "There's no time. You heard her. *Take care of him.*" Chet's eyes were wet and pleading.

Sam didn't answer. Couldn't answer. The pain was insurmountable.

Chet stared at him, pleading, and whispered, "Please, Sam. Take care of Jacob." He squeezed Sam's shoulder, kissed the boy on the head, and got up and ran to Yellow Teeth's mangled body. Quickly, he dug through the dead man's pockets until he found the keys to the Jeep.

Chet turned back one last time. "GO!" he yelled, and then set off running for the Jeep.

The crit had finished with its fourth and final victim. It turned to Sam and Jacob, taking a step toward them. The gunshots had torn it up and Sam could see it faltered slightly on one of its six legs.

He knew it wouldn't matter.

He saw Jacob stand in front of him and raise his hands, pushing like he had before. But his hands shook violently. His face was strained with sweat and exhaustion. The crit was unperturbed. It took another step.

We're going to die, Sam thought distractedly.

Chet dove into the Jeep and revved the engine to life.

"Hey!" he yelled, pounding on the horn. "Over here!" The crit snapped its head toward the Jeep, lunging for it just as Chet slammed on the accelerator. He took off southeast, away from Sam and Jacob, the crit right on his tail.

Sam knew it was now or never.

He looked down at his wife, his partner, the other half of him, and laid her head down gently. "I love you," he whispered. "I'm sorry."

Then he wiped his eyes, picked up the supplies he could carry, and turned to Jacob. His heart was breaking. He felt like a traitor, leaving her here. For making her ever leave their apartment. He felt like a fraud carrying on without her. But keeping this boy alive had been her one, last wish. And he'd be damned if he didn't grant it.

"Come on, kid," he said. "Let's go."

2074

Then

JACOB

AT FIRST, THEY JUST WALKED.

Months and months and months of walking through this place that looked like home, but wasn't. There were only five of them left and the two oldest among them were barely even teenagers. Jacob had never been alone with a group of kids like this and no adults, and it was strange. They'd set out with all the food they could gather up after the crash, but they stopped for things that looked edible as often as they could. The older kids seemed to have a general sense of where they were going, but not Jacob. He was so afraid in this new place without his parents, he felt like talking less and less. Most of the time he was thinking about his mom.

Jacob didn't know why they were here or why they'd had to leave home so quickly. He didn't understand anything except that they were trying to get somewhere and that his parents were gone and that this place had monsters, too.

They made a small fire one night and Paul came over to sit next to him.

"How are you doing?" Paul asked.

Jacob shrugged.

"I'm worried about you," Paul said. "This whole not talking thing."

"I'm just sad," Jacob answered. "I miss my mom and dad."

"I know," Paul replied. "I miss mine too."

"What do you think happened to yours?" Jacob asked.

Paul sighed. "I think they were heroes," he said, his voice breaking. He looked at Jacob with tears in his eyes. "Just like yours."

Jacob nodded. "I know they were," he said, hoping to make Paul feel better.

Paul smiled. "I'll watch out for you," he said. "Everything is going to be okay."

. . .

The next morning on their walk, some of the other kids found a ball laying in the street. It was different from the ones Jacob had at home, but it was still a ball. They started kicking it to each other and laughing and probably getting too loud, but it was the first time Jacob remembered smiling in weeks.

It was short-lived.

Out of the darkness, they heard a chittering noise. The same one Jacob had heard that last night at his mom's office.

"Shit," Paul muttered. "Get ready!"

The kids formed a line—most of them had never come face to face with one before, but Jacob had seen what Paul did to that one in that hallway.

"What do we do?" someone whispered.

"Hands up, just like you were taught," Paul said. "You know what to do, and you can do it."

Jacob was terrified. He could hear the massive, spidery legs hurtling closer and closer to them. He raised his hands.

"Here it comes!" Paul shouted.

The monster flew out of the darkness, bearing down on them at full speed. Jacob's heart jumped into his throat, but he was ready—or at least, he thought he was. He opened his hands, palms facing the monster, and focused on one thought: *stop*. He could feel the energy buzzing from all the kids around him, all of them focusing together, as one.

He almost couldn't believe it when the monster stopped running. It looked like it was being held back by a pair of invisible arms, it was *straining* to reach them, but it couldn't move. Jacob breathed out, and all together, they *pushed*.

The monster launched through the air, flailing its disgusting legs, landing in front of a nearby building.

"Run!" Paul shouted.

They all turned and sprinted as hard as they could in the opposite direction. Some were laughing in shock at what they'd all just done. Their lessons in school had been nothing like the real thing.

They didn't stick around long enough to see if the monster got up, which meant they didn't stick around to see a small blonde woman poking her head out from behind a building, her mouth hanging open, her piercing eyes full of greed.

2076

Now

Rory

She enjoys walking next to Jacob, speaking sometimes but mainly sharing the silence together. She is still in awe of him—of his powers, of course, but also of his resilience. What had he been through before meeting Sam?

Ahead, she sees that Sarah and Sam have stopped. They're staring at something in the distance. The moon has filled out to give them better light than they've had in days, yet Rory can see nothing. But she knows Sarah's eyesight. She feels for her rifle, brings it to her shoulder, and clicks the safety off in one sweeping motion.

She feels something brush her left side and looks down. Jacob's small, mittened hand reaches up toward her. Rory takes it.

"What is it?" she asks them when she's within a few yards, heart hammering.

But Sarah turns to her with huge eyes and smiles. "Mom," she says, pointing into the distance. "*Look.*"

She follows Sarah's gaze.

Her fear instantly abates. Nearly twenty years later and cloaked in darkness, but the view still takes her breath away.

Huge arches of dirt and rock dot the land before them, the frozen desert floor sprawling out under the night sky. Above them, there are a million stars. In the moonlight, the dirt's red hue is just visible, or maybe that's just how she remembers it.

Arches National Park. She knew they'd get here eventually if her navigation was correct. The only other time she'd been here was at eighteen, with Matt. It is one of her most precious memories. She'd been nervous to taint it with the darkness of this new world, but she knew Sarah would love it here. Being here also means they're close to the town where they can hopefully make a supply run tomorrow.

"This is so cool," Sarah says. "How did those get here?"

"Basically, centuries of erosion," Sam answers. "I can't believe they're still here—with how much everything's changed."

"Can we stop here tonight?" Sarah asks.

Rory smiles. "Yeah, we have to. Tomorrow, we've got to walk into town and see if we have a shot at finding some supplies."

Sarah's smile falters, but she nods.

Sam stiffens.

"Is that absolutely necessary?" he asks.

Rory knows the prospect of running into others is hard for him after the tragedy he's suffered, but it's hard for them all.

"We're out of food," she says.

"I can hunt."

"There's nothing out here to hunt. And we need to see if we can find water," she answers, not unkindly. "We're in the middle of a frozen desert with almost nothing to drink. And we'll need warmer clothes as we head north. Then we have to look for medicine, antibiotics, anything in case someone gets sick. We're walking all the way to Canada in the dark, Sam."

"It's not safe," he says. There's a distinct fear in his eyes she hasn't seen before.

"We have no choice," she sighs. "You don't have to come. Why don't you and Sarah—"

"I'm coming," he says, eyes narrowing.

"Okay," Rory answers. "We leave in the morning."

That night, for the first time in a long time, Rory gets to watch Sarah be a kid as they explore the park together. When she'd been here with Matt, the ground was made up of a soft, red dust. Now, it's rock solid. Frozen, like everything else. But the sky is incredible. As much time as they'd spent outside, Rory had never seen stars so spectacular. For once, it just feels like they are on a road trip together. Like there are no bad people or crits or constant darkness. This night is just as she'd hoped it would be when she decided to stop here. When they're officially worn out, they share a dinner of trail mix. It's all they have left, but somehow they feel full after it.

When they wake in the morning, Rory wants nothing more than to stay in this park forever.

2076

Now

Sam

Sam lies awake, thinking about their upcoming trip to town. The thought of any one of them getting hurt is unbearable.

Rory stirs next to him, and he sees that her eyes are open.

"Can't sleep?" he says.

"I never sleep."

"I'm sorry about yesterday," he says after a moment. "Going into towns…with Jacob," he takes a breath. "I have to get him to Canada safely."

"I get it," she says. "Every time we have to do this, I wonder if it's safer to leave her somewhere and go into the town alone, but…"

"But that means leaving her unprotected."

"Exactly," Rory nods. "Let's get in, find what we need, and get out."

He nods and a thought lingers between them. *It may not be that simple.*

Sam watches as Rory eases out of her sleeping bag and crawls over to wake Sarah. All of them sleep fully clothed now. The cold is unyielding.

When they're all awake and as full as they can be on the

last few crumbs of trail mix, they pack up and go over their emergency plans with Sarah and Jacob. But as they head for town, Sam can't shake his sense of dread.

. . .

What remains of the town of Moab sits in silent ruin in the middle of the desert. Huge dinosaur sculptures stand sentinel at the outskirts of town along the highway, and Sam finds it easy to picture the ancient creatures roaming here. Had they felt as he did now when they realized the world as they knew it was ending? Or had it truly just happened in a flash? And if so, was that a better way to go? No fear, no hope. Just gone in an instant.

The streets are empty but for a few stray, skeletal animals. They, too, looking for scraps of food. A coyote slinks down the street a few yards from them, nose to the ground, stopping to sniff every few feet. The animal has no fear of them, Sam realizes. It, like them, has seen far worse out here.

To Sam's left, the "R" on the sign for the Moab Diner dangles pathetically, hanging by a single electrical cord. A few cars are still parked in the parking lot. Some have been completely trampled by crits. Some look so normal Sam can almost imagine their owners are inside finishing breakfast.

To their right, they spot a sign for Moab Gear Trader.

"First stop," Rory whispers.

Inside, the place has been ransacked, and though they'd expected as much, Sam's heart still sinks at the sight. The door has been knocked completely off its hinges, the front window smashed in, and broken glass covers the floors. Snapped clothing racks lay in heaps and the shelves are all but depleted. This will take longer than they'd hoped, if they can find anything at all.

Even though it's freezing, Sam realizes he's sweating. His heart is racing.

"Sam and Jacob," Rory whispers, "you're on accessories; gloves, hats, socks, whatever you can find. We'll take sweat-shirts and—"

There is a loud crash behind them. Sam and Rory have their guns drawn in an instant.

An emaciated raccoon races out from behind a toppled shelf and sprints for the door. Sam feels himself release a breath he hadn't realized he was holding.

He looks at the others.

"Okay," he says, taking a deep breath to center himself. "Quickly."

They split up and begin searching through the wreckage, shoving whatever they can find into their packs. Sam has better luck than he thought; it seems as though most people have only scavenged for tools. He finds insulated mittens, wool socks, and even a couple of fur-lined hats with ear flaps. This place must have restocked once the dark started expanding years ago. Most of what he finds is too big or too small, but it will work nonetheless.

They reconvene after what seems like an hour, but is really less than fifteen minutes. When he sees that Rory and Sarah's hands and bags are also full, he sends a thank you up to the powers that be—whatever they are.

He meets Rory's gaze and they nod at each other to confirm they have what they need.

Time for stop number two.

They find the pharmacy in a similar state, but here, people

have targeted the necessities: drugs. Bottles litter the ground and pills crunch under Sam's boots as he tries to navigate the debris, searching for anything that could be useful.

The electricity went out long ago, but a rectangular fluorescent light fixture hangs eerily from the ceiling. If he closes his eyes, Sam can picture tourists here stocking up on blister pads, Advil, and snacks before heading out to explore the national parks. The sun would've been shining. Parents would've been with their children, spouses would've been holding hands, all heading out to enjoy their vacations.

He pushes the thought away. No point.

They approach the pharmacy counter slowly, warily, and as they get closer, Sam sees a single, overturned boot poking out from behind it. He freezes and raises a hand, signaling them all to stop. His senses are on fire. He listens, but hears nothing.

Taking another step forward, he sees that the boot is attached to a leg. He moves silently, gun at the ready, though he knows what's coming when he peers behind the drugstore counter.

The dead man stares straight up, his mouth open in surprise, his skin pale. He is maybe forty-five years old with brown hair and months' worth of beard on his face. Three bullet holes pierce his coat, and a pool of frozen, gelatin blood has stained the white floor beneath him. Sam looks around, not daring to breathe, *listening*. But still, there is nothing but silence.

He waves Rory forward, but Sarah approaches faster and sees the dead man. Sam realizes it isn't the first dead body the girl has seen.

Who was he? Sam thinks. *Who killed him?*

And though he tries to push one last, chilling thought away before they begin their search of the pharmacy, he can't.

He hasn't been dead long.

With some digging, they find Tylenol, vitamin C tablets, bandages, and a single bottle of amoxicillin—Sam says another silent prayer that no one will need it as they head for the exit. One more stop and they'll be on their way.

The main road through Moab is miles of desolation. This town had once been a tourist hub, most people using it as a jumping point for the national parks. Everywhere they look, there are signs of the horrors that have taken place here. They wade through the wreckage, climbing over piles of trash, loose clothing, and abandoned vehicles. As they make their way through the town, Sam sees a tiny yellow toddler's shoe cast aside in the street. A chill runs through him.

Even though the town is deserted, he can't shake the feeling that they are being watched.

The sign for the Village Market is dark as they approach, its lights having shut off long ago. Shopping carts have been strewn about the parking lot and the silence here is deafening. Sam still feels strange in places like grocery stores—places that had once been packed with irritable shoppers, but are now deserted. He'd hated grocery shopping before The Collapse. And now he'd give anything just to go one more time.

Someone had propped the once-automatic doors open, and as they step warily inside, Rory and Sam exchange a look. He can read Rory's eyes in one second, because he feels the same way.

Be careful, those eyes say. *This has been too easy.*

This store is enormous, so they decide to stay together here rather than splitting up. They only need two things: any non-perishable food they can find and water.

The interior of the store is a ruin. Racks toppled over onto each other, debris scattered everywhere, and stray clothing strewn about at random. Sam strains his ears and hears nothing, but the darkness in the back of the store is ominous. *Someone is watching us,* he thinks, over and over again. He thinks of the dead man, his mouth an "O" of surprise. He pushes the thought away again.

"Okay," Rory whispers to them. "Water."

They turn to head in what they hope is the right direction, but for a moment, Jacob doesn't move. His green eyes are turned toward the darkness of the back of the store. Sam feels goosebumps rise up on his neck.

"What is it?" he asks, barely a whisper.

Jacob wrenches his eyes away to look at Sam and says nothing.

"Rory," Sam says, trying to get her attention. But she is too far away. The knot in Sam's stomach tightens. *Breathe,* he tells himself. *Just fucking breathe. You've seen worse than whatever's back there.* That one thought propels him forward.

Ahead, Sam can see Rory bent over something—water. Four five-gallon jugs laid on the floor in front of them. After so much time in this cold, the jugs are mostly ice. But Rory is cutting the plastic off and picking at the giant ice blocks so they can stow away enough to melt it. It's too loud. But there's no other choice. They have to move faster.

He joins her, following suit, filling his own water bladder as well as Jacob's. *Faster, faster, faster.* Jacob is too small to carry the weight of what he'll need, so he carries what he can, but Sam carries most of it. To his right, Sarah is loading their bags with any food she can get her hands on. The store still has some canned goods—nothing they'll enjoy much, but at least it's something.

We're gonna make it, Sam allows himself to think as he caps the now-full water bladders. *We're gonna fucking make it.*

To his right, he hears a crunch. For one second, he thinks Sarah has stepped on glass with her boot, but out of the corner of his eye, he sees that Jacob has frozen.

His hand goes to his gun. There is a flurry of motion. As if from under water, he hears Rory shout, "No!"

He spins around. A group of four men stand to his right, one of them with his arms around a squirming Sarah, holding her around the neck. Her eyes are huge with panic. Sam's heart goes into his throat. The memories flood back to him in horrifying detail.

Becca.

These men are exactly like the others. The ones from that night. They have the same deranged look in their black eyes—something animalistic that took over long ago. Their skin is pale, their beards wild and unkempt, and they are strapped to the teeth with weapons. What stands out to Sam—as it always has—is their confidence. They *know* they'll get what they want, whatever it is.

"Out for a shopping spree, eh?" says the one in front. He is smaller than the others, with a huge tattoo running from his neck up to his eye. His hair is laden with grease. His cracked lips surround a dark hole full of rotting teeth.

"Let her go," Rory says, her voice surprisingly even. Even from here, Sam can see her breath. Sarah lets out a muffled sob, and Sam registers Rory's whole body shaking. Rory takes a step forward.

The man holding Sarah takes out a knife and touches it to her throat. "Not so fast," Tattoo Face says, grinning. "Let's all just calm down for a second, eh? Don't want to do anything we regret."

"Let her go," Rory says again, this time her voice shakes on the last syllable.

"She yours, then?" the man says with a smile.

Rory says nothing.

"Well, you should know better than to bring a girl this pretty into a town like this," Tattoo Face says. "Tell you what, we'll take her and let the rest of you leave, okay? We'll find plenty of use for her."

The one holding Sarah runs his hands down the front of her teenage body, over her breasts, her stomach, her hips. She thrashes in his grasp, his knife so close to her throat it's nicked her, drawing blood.

It's then that Sam notices Sarah's right hand—it's moving, slowly, toward her pocket.

Rory's body seems to vibrate. "I won't say it again," she says. "Let her go."

Sam's mind is racing. He gauges the situation from every angle. He could shoot, but what if he misses? There are four of them. What if the knife slips and Rory has to watch Sarah bleed out? He thinks of Becca again. He doesn't move.

Just as he is about to speak, a rack falls over somewhere in the darkness behind the men.

Then several things happen at once.

The man holding Sarah turns his head at the sound, and as he does, his knife drops just an inch. Sarah grabs his arm with one hand and pushes the knife just far enough away from her throat to spin and slip under his arm. Sam sees a glint of silver in Sarah's other hand and she stabs it, in quick succession, into her attacker's ribcage, *one, two, three.* He lets out a bubbly shriek of agony and drops the knife, falling to his knees.

Before Tattoo Face has time to turn around and see what happened, Sam re-aims his rifle, firing once. He hits his target in the right temple, and the man crumples to the ground in a heap.

Sarah sprints back to them, they grab their bags, and run.

The store explodes around them. Sam hears the shelves crash down around them, sending stale bread and gallons of old milk flying as they flee for cover.

"Mom!" Sarah shouts.

"Keep moving!" Rory answers.

Sam's heart threatens to rip through his chest as they sprint through the store. He holds tight to Jacob's hand and scans every wall for somewhere to hide.

They hear the screaming, the tearing flesh, and the *chittering* behind them. Sam's vision swims with the familiarity of this situation. He can't lose any of them. Not again. And he knows the crit will come for them next.

"There!" Rory shouts, veering to the left. "The closet!"

She yanks open the door to a storage closet and they dive inside, slamming it shut behind them.

There is a muffled gurgling sound in the distance. Sam has heard enough men die to know what it means.

Time ticks by slowly, none of them dare to even breathe too loudly. Sam looks down and realizes Sarah has a vice grip on her mother's hand. The girl is shaking from head to toe, but her face is resolute.

She didn't fall apart. And in the moment, she'd been ready. Calm. Focused. Prepared.

Finally, they hear the crit moving through the store. More shelves crash and bags burst open. But the one, unmistakable sound is that of six legs clicking across the linoleum. Sam and Rory both have their guns in hand, ready for whatever comes through the door.

It's getting closer.

Jacob's eyes are steady, unblinking. He stares at the door. Sam sees the child flex his palms.

The sound of those legs draws nearer and nearer, until finally, they stop—right outside the closet door. They can hear it then, *sniffing*, searching for them. It scratches the door with a spidery leg.

This is it, Sam thinks. None of them move. Jacob keeps staring.

But nothing happens. The door remains shut. After the longest minute of Sam's life, it shuffles away, leaving them alone in the darkness.

They sit in that closet for a long time, well after the crit has gone. Each one shaking, thinking about how close it had been. Only when they are sure it's safe do they—Rory first—pick up their belongings and do the only thing they can do.

They keep moving.

2072

Then

Rory

THE LAST THEY SAW OF PIERCE WAS HER EMPTY SMILE, then the doors banged shut.

"What do we do?" Susan cried. She held one of her sons and looked at Nick, who held the other. He was drenched in sweat. His eyes bulged out of his head.

Rory's brain worked fast. She searched the room for doors, windows, anything that could serve as an escape route. Every exit was blocked, guarded by armed soldiers. *Why doesn't anyone think that's strange?* She thought to herself.

Because we believe what we want to believe.

"There," Matt pointed.

Rory followed his gaze.

Behind one of the ships, Matt had spotted the window where Nick had watched the extermination unfold just days ago. It was hidden. The guards would have a hard time seeing them. If they could just get to it without attracting any attention…

It was their only hope.

Rory nodded and took one step toward the window.

"It's a trap!" Nick suddenly screamed, trying to be heard

over the sound of hundreds of people. "We have to get out of here!"

Matt grabbed his friend, "shut *up*," he hissed. "Let's get to the window. If you cause a scene—"

But Nick couldn't hear him, couldn't see him. His eyes were filled with terror. He was gone. "RUN!" Nick shrieked, "THEY'RE GOING TO KILL US ALL! RUN—"

Rory slapped him across the face hard enough to split his lip. But it was too late.

"What is he talking about?" she heard someone say, as if from a distance.

"The ships don't go anywhere!" Nick said. "We've seen it—they're going to kill us! We have to *do* something!"

"Mommy," Billy yelled, sobbing. "What's happening?"

Slowly, people started to look at their surroundings. They took in the armed guards with their masks near the doors. Then they began to realize.

"Excuse me?" a man said to one of the guards. "Excuse me—we're—my family and I are leaving," he said.

The guard didn't answer. Didn't move.

Another man tried with another guard. He was met with the same response.

Rory watched eyes turn to saucers, watched parents pull their children close.

"What's going on here?" a woman near them said.

"I said my family and I are leaving," said the first man again, this time to another guard. He made to push past.

Like swatting a fly, the guard smacked the man across the face with the butt of his rifle. There was an audible *crunch* as the man's nose shattered, spraying blood, and he fell to the floor. His wife screamed.

"None of you are going anywhere," the guard said.

Panic surged through the crowd. Rory and Matt looked at each other, and she'd never forget what passed between them. Somehow, she'd think later, they both knew. This would be their last day together. But they had one shared thought: *Sarah.*

"WE HAVE TO GET OUT OF HERE!" Nick screamed.

She felt Matt's hand on her arm. "We have to move," he said.

The pitch of the crowd rose, heading toward pandemonium. The guards had stepped away from the doors, hands on their rifles, beating down anyone who tried to get by.

"The window," Matt said, grabbing Sarah's hand. "It's our only chance."

By the time they reached the window, the room was in a full-blown riot. Rory could hear the guard's radios but knew she didn't have time to stop and listen. She looked back in Nick and Susan's direction, but couldn't see them anywhere. *Don't think about that now,* she thought. *Get your family out of here.*

The window was locked. Matt took off his jacket, tied it around his arm, and smashed through it. The noise was nothing over the sound of the crowd inside the arena.

And then she heard it. The *hiss* as the gas came on.

"Oh my God, Matt," she said. "The gas," her panic was rising.

He grabbed her shoulders and shook her. "Rory," he said. "Climb!"

It was enough to snap her back into action and in one swift motion, she'd pulled herself up and out the small window, landing in a hallway, and reached back for Sarah. As Matt lifted their daughter, they heard gunshots—three, in rapid succession.

Pop pop pop.

The sound jolted Matt so hard he nearly lost his grip on Sarah and began to turn around.

"Come on!" Rory shouted from just outside—her arms reaching out for Sarah. She grabbed her daughter and pulled, leaning her head inside. What she saw, she would remember forever. She could already taste the gas. It was bitter, suffocating. Susan must've just breached the crowd and tried to follow them, and now her friend's body lay in a pool of blood on the ground behind Matt. Two smaller bodies were beside her. They could've been sleeping.

"Oh my God," she whispered. "Oh Jesus Christ…" her hands started to shake.

"Rory!" Matt yelled, choking with every breath in. "*Take her!*" He shoved Sarah through the window, she and Rory tumbling back into a long hallway. Rory righted herself and ran back to help Matt, who had started to pull himself out.

"Hey!" shouted a voice behind him. "What do you think you're doing?"

"Matt," Rory said, eyeing the guard behind him, nausea threatening to upend her lunch. "Move." She grabbed for any purchase to help him through the window.

"Stop!" said the voice from behind, muffled under the mask. "I will fucking shoot you!"

As fast as he could, Matt pulled himself up onto the sill, tearing the bottom of his shirt on glass and scratching his stomach as he tried to hoist himself out. Rory held half of his weight on her shoulders as he came down, just able to see the armed soldier behind him grab him around the waist.

"Get off him!" she screamed.

Matt fell back into the room, the gas just visible now. People nearer to the vents started to choke.

She saw that when the guard tackled Matt, he'd dropped his gun. They were both crawling for it now.

"Go!" he screamed to her. But she couldn't move.

"MATT!" she heard herself yell.

Her husband's finger tips grazed the rifle, then he got a full hand around it. The guard had grabbed his legs, Matt squirmed in his grasp. Rory couldn't breathe.

"Fuck OFF!" Matt screamed. In one, fluid motion, he bludgeoned the side of the guard's helmet with the butt of the rifle, dislodging his gas mask. The guard panicked, reaching for it and forgetting Matt.

"Come on!" Rory shouted.

Matt threw the gun through the window before yanking himself up, choking on gas as he did.

But they'd made it.

The hallway was empty, but they could hear commotion coming from all sides.

"Let's go this way," Matt said, picking up the rifle. "Quickly."

"How do we know there aren't more waiting for us?" Rory asked.

"We don't," he said.

Rory grabbed Sarah's hand and the three of them bolted through the hallways, which seemed endless. There were cameras everywhere, and Rory kept thinking she could hear someone on their tail.

"This way!" Matt yelled up ahead, even though none of them knew where they were going.

Finally, they saw exit signs emerging. Rory's lungs were on fire and her legs felt like they would give out any second. They were nearly there. They would make it.

But then Matt rounded a corner a few steps ahead of them.

"Freeze!" a voice screamed, right as a gunshot went off.

Rory yanked Sarah's hand back and flattened them both against the wall, out of sight.

No no no please God no.

Her hands shook. Even though she was out of breath, she held it.

"Mom?" Sarah whispered.

"I'm okay," Matt's voice came from ahead. "I'm…okay."

Rory lunged around the corner. There was a dead guard on the floor, blood blooming on his shirt. Matt's hands shook as he clutched the smoking rifle.

He looked at her for a long time. She squeezed his hand.

"We need to go," she whispered. "Now."

. . .

The streets were madness. Word had spread like wildfire about the crowd they'd driven over on their way in, and now people were mobbing the gates of the arena. It was clear that some version of the truth was out.

In the last few weeks, the darkness had expanded rapidly. So rapidly that it could be seen to make huge progress over the span of a single day. The wall that had eaten their tax dollars for decades was useless, lost to the darkness years ago. Rory saw people sprinting through the streets—the darkness drawing a swift line through the city. A line that was even closer now than yesterday. As people ran, they shoved others over the line and into the dark. She heard the screams from the other side. She saw—for just a moment—a furry, insect-like leg reached out into the light, only to hear a screeching sound as it recoiled.

"Mom!" Sarah screamed. "What *was* that?"

"I don't know, honey," she said, looking at Matt. His eyes were huge.

Her best friend's body lying face down, her children beside her—

The sound of glass smashing to her right anchored her back to the present moment and she watched the front window of a Radio Shack burst open. A crowd ran inside and grabbed what they could, fighting if they had to.

There was a series of gunshots somewhere close by.

Pop pop pop pop.

Susan. Billy. Andrew.

"We have to keep moving," Matt said.

Matt grabbed Sarah's hand and they made a run for a nearby parking lot, hoping they'd get lucky and find a car with keys in it.

They tried at least ten cars before Matt finally yelled that he'd found one with a set of keys. It was an old, white Nissan. They clambered into the car and Matt stomped on the accelerator.

. . .

Their neighborhood was quieter, but they knew it wouldn't be long. Their neighbors had stood by and watched them being dragged away just this morning. Rory looked down and saw that her hands were shaking. She couldn't get them to stop.

When they pulled into the driveway, her nausea won out. She opened the passenger side door and vomited onto the front lawn.

"Mom!" Sarah yelled. "Are you okay?"

"I'm okay, honey," she said. "You need to go inside right now and get your suitcase, okay?"

Matt came over and rubbed her back. "We can't stay here," he said. "What if she comes back?"

"I know," Rory said, wiping her mouth. "But we have time. She thinks we're dead, remember?" She looked up at their house, eyes struggling to focus—it wasn't much, but it was their home. She'd spent years planting and tending to the garden out front, showing Sarah how to take care of the plants and help them survive longer in the constant sunlight. She knew that soon, all of the plants would wither up in the darkness. The thought broke her heart.

The porch swing moved idly in the breeze. Two pillows rested on it, both of which her mother had crocheted for her when she was a teenager. This was the house she and Matt had lived in since their first year of marriage, the house they'd raised Sarah in—the only home Sarah had ever known. Rory never imagined this was how they'd leave. She vomited again.

Matt reached over and squeezed her hand. "Twenty minutes," he said gently. "I don't like the idea of sticking around."

She nodded, swiping at a tear in her eye, wiping her mouth again.

They'd had their bags packed for days, thinking they were getting on the next ship. Rory steadied herself before going inside. She had a daughter—she needed to pull it the fuck together.

When she was sure she wouldn't vomit again, she went inside and hurried around the house, grabbing any food she thought would last, and even some that she knew wouldn't. Matt had dug their old camel backs out and was filling them in the sink. *What the hell are we doing?* Rory kept thinking to herself. But she knew this was it—this was really happening. It wasn't something they could put off.

So she kept moving, because she knew she had to.

2076

Now

Sarah

She has only ever been that scared one other time in her life, Sarah thinks the day after the trip into Moab. But she's also never felt so satisfied—her training actually paid off in her moment of need. She'd been terrified, and still, she'd fought back and gotten away.

"You did great," her mom says as they walk. "I mean, Jesus, it scared the shit out of me, but I'm so proud of you."

Sarah needs to hear it. Her pride swells. She feels, for the first time in her life, less afraid. Less in need of protection. Less like prey, more like predator.

"Thank Sam for all the training," she says. "It was like—even though I was scared—I just remembered that I knew what to do, you know?"

"That's exactly what I wanted you to get out of all that training," her mom says. "You were right, after all. About us needing them."

Sarah raises her eyebrows. "I'm sorry?" she says, laughing. "'I was *right*' and 'we *need them*'?"

Her mom smiles. "Well, don't tell *them* that."

Sarah shoves her mom with an elbow. "It's nice having them around, isn't it?"

"I can't believe it," her mom answers. "But yes, it is."

Sarah had been high all day on the adrenaline of her escape, but now she really looks at her mother. Her face is ashen, her scar more prominent than ever. Her hands shake.

"Are you okay, Mom?" she asks.

Her mother smiles weakly, squeezing her hand. "I'm okay," she says. "I just…the thought of what could've happened…"

"But it didn't."

"I know, but it was too close. If anything ever happened to you…I don't know what I'd do."

Sarah squeezes her mom's hand back.

"I'm okay, Mom," she says. "I'm not a kid anymore. I can take care of myself."

Her mom laughs. "I know that," she says. "But you're still *my* kid. I'm always going to worry about you."

"I know," Sarah says. They walk in silence for a few moments. "I think we're going to make it to Canada." Sarah says. "I can feel it."

"You know what?" her mom says. "I think we are, too."

It is the first time in two years that Sarah remembers feeling hopeful. They are getting closer to Calgary each day, sure. But more than anything, she's hopeful for a new life with the people she can finally call family.

2076

Now

Rory

"I should've listened to you," Rory says a few days later as she walks next to Sam. They'd left Moab quickly and quietly and had no further trouble, but still, it had been too close. Of course she was grateful that their bags were stocked with supplies, but at what cost? Every night since, she's dreamed of those men taking Sarah away.

She sees that next to her, Sam is smiling.

"What?" Rory asks.

"It's not often a woman has admitted that to me in my life," Sam says. "And you don't strike me as the kind of woman to admit you were wrong easily."

"I know how I can be," Rory says, "but it's because I *have* to be."

"Trust me," Sam says seriously. "I know."

"I just—I can't stop thinking about..." Rory trails off

Sam glances at her. "She was good," he says. "Sarah. She was great, actually. You should be proud."

Rory scoffs. "I *am*," she says. "It's the what ifs that are killing me. How could I have let that happen?"

"Hey," he says, turning to her. "You didn't *let* anything

happen. It's no one's fault but those scumbags'. "

"But I'm the one who promised her father I'd protect her," Rory says, exhaling. She looks ahead to her daughter, who is walking with Jacob. She can tell Sarah is talking with him and wonders what they're saying. Then she blinks, and there is Sarah again, knife at her throat, looking to Rory for help. Her hands start to shake.

"Rory," Sam says. He stops, turns to her, and puts both hands on her shoulders. "There are things in this world you can't protect her from. That's why I wanted to train her to fight. In this world, darkness or light, it doesn't matter. A girl needs to know how to protect herself. You know that."

Rory stares at him. "I'm sorry about what happened to you," she says. "Can I ask what she was like?"

"My wife?" Sam asks.

Rory nods.

"Becca…she was smart. And hilarious," Sam says. "One of the funniest people I've ever met. Even when things started to really go to shit, she never lost that sense of humor. But eventually, it got pretty hard," he gestures around himself. "I think, in the end, Jacob was a huge help in getting her back to herself—even if she wasn't around him very long." His voice breaks.

Rory nods.

"She gave her life for him," Sam goes on. "I really think that, in some way, she knew he was our best hope. Maybe just because she saw his ability to bring people back to themselves, I don't know. But she knew he'd be important."

Rory is silent. She knows it's been Sarah who's kept her tethered to herself—who's kept her going.

"And honestly," Sam continues. "If it weren't for that little boy, I wouldn't have stuck around either." He looks toward Jacob, who is clearly smiling at whatever Sarah is saying to him. "I would've found some way to…"

He doesn't have to finish.

"I can't believe I'm saying this," Rory says, "but I'm glad you're with us."

Sam smiles for a moment, and then it fades. "I have to tell you both something tonight," he says. "And after I do, I'm not sure you'll want us around anymore."

"What are you talking about?" Rory says.

"When we make camp, I'll explain everything."

2075-2076

Then

Sam

THE WEEKS AFTER LOSING BECCA were the worst of Sam's life. He would never have carried on if it weren't for Jacob. And Sam knew that the kid was hurting, too. He'd hoped that night within a few hours, they may see headlights in the distance—a sign of Chet coming back to them. But he knew it was hopeless. It was just the two of them now.

They spent a few months in an abandoned hunting cabin they'd stumbled upon a few days after the attack. Sam knew they should keep moving, but the reality was that he couldn't. Beyond their devastation, they were exhausted and hungry. They'd reached a low point he didn't know was possible. Every night he woke up in a terror, gasping for air. Jacob would run to him and try to calm him down as best he could, but the realization of waking up in a world without Becca hit Sam like a gut punch every time. He and Jacob had both seen too much out on the road.

But he knew they had no choice but to keep moving.

Take care of him, Becca had said. And he knew the best way to do that was to get him, safely, to Canada.

So one morning, after gathering what supplies they could from the cabin, they walked on.

Most days passed in a cold, silent blur. His thoughts of Becca threatened to overwhelm him, but he told himself he'd be free as soon as he delivered the boy to Calgary. Then, maybe, he could disappear.

One morning as they trekked through northern Utah, Jacob spoke.

"I miss my family, too," he said.

Sam had been lost in thought and nearly jumped at the sound. He turned to look at Jacob.

"Where is your family?" Sam asked.

"Gone," Jacob said.

"I'm sorry," Sam answered.

Jacob reached up and grabbed Sam's hand, squeezing it through their mittens.

"I'm sorry, too," he said quietly.

It was the first crack through Jacob's brick walls, Sam thought. And maybe, he realized, through his too. Over the next few weeks, they talked more and more. Jacob didn't speak much, but Sam tried, gently, to coax some of his story out. He remembered Chet's advice—just keep talking, and eventually, you'll get something. He learned that Jacob's family had clearly perished during the last few years, and he'd spent some time, it seemed, with some other kids. But they'd been separated.

"What happened?" Sam asked.

"Her," Jacob said.

"Who?"

"The cold woman."

Sam had no idea what to make of this. "Who is the cold woman, Jacob?"

The boy looked down, walking in silence. Sam figured the conversation was over.

"She hurt my friends," Jacob finally said.

"Why?" Sam asked.

"I don't know," he said. "And I don't know where they are now."

"Were they friends from school?" Sam asked, trying to probe for information without pushing too far.

"No," Jacob said. "From home."

Each time Sam sought clarity from Jacob, he ended up more confused. But he learned, at least, that people had loved this boy and he had loved them back. And that was something worth fighting for.

He had no idea that soon enough the cold woman would find them.

Then

Jacob

They ran so fast and so far, Jacob thought his lungs would burst. Over the months they'd been walking, they'd found some clothing to add on themselves so that they could stay warm, and it was hard to move in all the layers. But running this fast made him warm for the first time he could remember since being home.

He was terrified the monster was following them, but didn't dare turn around. Paul was still clenching his hand, dragging him nearly hard enough to tear his arm off, but he was slowing down. When they finally approached a small stand of trees, Paul led them all into the brush to hide.

Jacob crouched low next to Paul, and when he looked up at his life-long friend, it was like he was seeing him for the first time. They'd grown up a lot over these months, and though Jacob wouldn't fully comprehend it for years to come, he was starting to realize the weight on Paul's shoulders— leading this group of kids and keeping them alive, just because he was the oldest. His face looked thinner, his mouth had started to set itself in a hard line, and he was constantly on alert. His childhood had been stamped out far too early.

They waited until they were sure the monster wasn't following them—either they really had killed it, or it was too scared to follow them—before they crept out of the trees and into a clearing to make a plan.

Paul knelt down to look at them. "Great job, you guys," he said. "I knew you could do it."

Some of the younger ones had used their powers before, but never like that. Most of them, like Jacob, had only had a few lessons in school before they left home.

"Now, I think it's time we started practicing more—" Paul started.

"Paul!" one of the other kids whispered. "Someone's coming."

Jacob whipped around and saw the outline of three people approaching. They were close. Too close to make a run for it.

"Everyone get behind me," Paul said, though Jacob could see the sweat on his brow. He could feel the exhaustion in his own body, too. Fighting off the crit had drained him.

As the three strangers got closer, the hair on the back of Jacob's neck started to stand up. It was a feeling he couldn't describe—but something deep inside him knew this was wrong. They couldn't trust these people. One glance at Paul told him his friend was feeling the same.

"Hello," one of them said. She had a slight limp and a voice that made him afraid. "My name is Pierce."

"What do you want?" Paul said.

The woman smiled. But it wasn't a real smile—it made Jacob shudder.

"We saw what you did back there," she said, pushing blonde hair out of her face. Jacob noticed the two men with her had something in their hands. They looked like weapons. "I think you could be helpful to us fighting off the crits."

That must be what they call them here, Jacob thought.

"We're not interested," Paul said.

"Oh? Why not?"

"We're looking for our friends."

A flash of greed in Pierce's eyes. "There are *more* of you?" she whispered. "Wonderful."

"I said we're not interested," Paul answered.

Pierce smiled again. "Unfortunately," she said. "We're not asking." Her men raised their guns.

"No!" One of the boys yelled.

The man to Pierce's right flew back almost 50 yards and hit the ground. The force was so sudden that the man to her left jumped nearly a foot off the ground, his rifle discharging at the same time.

Jacob heard Paul gasp and watched as his friend clutched the left side of his chest, going down hard on one knee.

"NO!" Pierce screamed. "You *idiot!*" she said, turning to the man on her left.

Jacob was frozen with shock. There was blood gushing out of Paul's chest—more blood than he'd ever seen. And still, he watched Paul raise his right palm toward their attackers. One final sacrifice for them all.

"RUN!" Paul shouted. Pierce and the man went flying, but the sound of Paul's voice shook Jacob into action. He turned and sprinted for his life.

He ran and ran and didn't stop running until his legs were like rocks and his lungs were on fire. And then he ducked behind a tree and hid, sure that the woman and those two men would appear at any minute. But they never did. And that's when he realized all the other children had run in different directions. He was alone.

He waited, crouching in those trees for hours until he finally stood up. His legs were stiff and he was thirsty. He looked around and heard nothing, so he decided to try and find his way back to that clearing.

It was a long time before he reached Paul. He looked around and saw no one, and then he ran to his friend. Paul had pitched forward and lay face down on the hard ground. It took some effort, but Jacob rolled him over to see if he was breathing. Paul's face was white as a sheet, his eyes were closed, and his lips were blue. Jacob remembered his mother—how he thought she was sleeping. He knew better now. This boy had taken care of them all for nearly a year, and now he was gone. It was too much. Why had they ever come here? He just wanted to go home.

But life on the road had taught him that there was no home. Not anymore. So instead, he wiped his tears, grabbed Paul's backpack full of supplies, slung it over his shoulder, and crept off into the darkness.

. . .

Jacob had learned how to blend in during his months out here. He'd learned how to find things to eat, how to build a fire, and how to quietly look for shelter. He'd been searching for a place where he could get a few nights of sleep when he came across the three new people.

The first time he heard them, they were sitting around a campfire chatting.

"Nights like these make me miss our boring life in that

apartment," the older man said, tucking his jacket tighter around himself. "Why the hell did you let me convince you to leave?"

The other two laughed. "Can I finally say 'I told you so'?" the woman answered.

"Never," said the older one, smiling.

"This place in Canada better have heat," the younger man said. "I'm starting to think I won't have any toes left when we get there."

Jacob had been thinking his toes were really cold, too.

"Oh come on," the woman answered him. "I'll keep your toes warm tonight."

"Jesus, now I really miss being in my own apartment," the old man said, and they all laughed.

Jacob leaned against a tree and listened to them all talk for a while. It was soothing. It reminded him of home, of the way his parents used to talk to each other. He didn't get that weird feeling about these people—that feeling that maybe they were bad. Instead, he felt the opposite. He wasn't anywhere near their fire, but he felt warm.

So he followed them. Day after day, stopping to listen to them when they'd make a fire just so he could hear the sound of their voices. Being with them felt like being part of a group again.

One day while he was following them, he watched them go into an old house. When they went inside, he waited in the field, ducking behind a bush so they wouldn't see him. From where he hid, he saw a Jeep drive up and a man jump out and go into the house. His heart jumped into his throat. Instantly, he heard shouting coming from inside and he felt himself start to freeze.

But then he thought of Paul, his friend's final act of bravery to keep the rest of them alive, and he knew what he had to do.

He wouldn't run away, not this time.

2076

Now

RORY

"IT WAS LATE AT NIGHT WHEN THEY FINALLY FOUND US," Sam says into the darkness. Rory and Sarah sit facing him silently, Jacob is quiet beside Sam.

"When who found you?" Rory asks.

"The day we met you two…we had so few supplies for a reason. This group…they crept up on us. I guess they'd followed Jacob for awhile—he ran into them somewhere a few months before he met me. I should've heard them, but I didn't," Sam lets out a long breath. "By the time we did hear them, it was too late. They told us to come out or they'd start shooting into the tent. Why would we think they were bluffing?"

Rory closes her eyes but says nothing.

"At that point," Sam says, "we were sleeping with our bags packed, so we grabbed them and brought them outside with us. I didn't know what else to do. Looking back, that decision saved our asses. At first, I figured they were looking for…" he looks sideways at Rory and Sarah.

"Women," Rory finishes.

"Yes," Sam says. "So I figured they'd kill us and move on. But once I got a good look at the three of them, I noticed that one of them *was* a woman. And they just didn't *look* like the others, you know? Like, crazy I guess. I could just tell immediately that this was something different. Something… organized. The two guys she was with were, I don't know, her guards or something—I mean, she was clearly the brains of the operation. She had this, like, platinum blonde hair. And there was just something…I don't know, *evil* about her."

Rory feels a chill go down her spine. *It's not possible.*

"She started asking all these questions about Jacob. Where I found him—she didn't believe for a second that he was my son—how long we'd been traveling together, shit like that. And I just knew then that she *knew* about him.

"She had her gun on me, and then the two guys with her made their move to take him. I…I thought I was going to lose him. But then, I heard him," Sam smiles. "Just like you did that night with the crit. 'No,' he said. And before I could even turn around, the two guys went flying thirty yards away from us."

Sarah smiles. And, Rory notices, so does Jacob.

"And when that woman turned her gun on him, the gun just…crumpled. Like it was a tin can. And the look on her face," Sam and Jacob look at each other. "Priceless. And then she was flying too, and Jacob and I grabbed our stuff and made a run for it," he finishes.

"What else did you notice about that woman?" Rory asks. "Anything else you can remember?"

Sam thinks for a moment. "She was walking with a limp. Not terrible, but definitely noticeable."

Rory's throat is dry.

"And honestly? The thing about her that freaked me out the most was her *smile*. It was just…empty."

Rory is silent for a long time. A million memories hit her like a wave.

Enjoy your trip.

"No," she whispers.

"I understand if you don't want us to stay," Sam says. "I know I may have put you both in danger. But they didn't follow us. I made sure of it. When I looked back, they were all unconscious."

"No, it's not that," Rory whispers.

Sam looks at her questioningly.

"That woman," Rory says. "She killed my husband."

2072

Then

RORY

RORY WAS STUFFING CANS OF BEANS AND TOMATO SOUP into her hiking backpack when she heard the front door open. She figured it was Matt grabbing something from the porch outside, so she continued emptying the cupboards.

Then she heard a muffled yell.

The soups clattered to the linoleum floor as she dropped them and ran for the living room.

But she was too late.

She'd never forget how out of place Pierce and her single guard looked standing in the middle of her living room, restraining her husband with a gun to his head. To her, it was just yesterday that she changed diapers on that sofa, or put Christmas gifts under the fake tree that always stood in the corner.

How did they find us so soon?

Pierce looked worse for wear. Her clothes were ragged. Her white suit was torn and stained with what looked like dirt and blood, and her perfectly groomed hair from earlier today now fell into her eyes.

Where is Sarah? Rory thought.

"Mass killings not go so well earlier, then?" Rory said, racking her brain for a way to distract Pierce—to keep her talking.

Pierce smiled without smiling. "Oh, it went fine for your friends," she hissed. "Now where is that beautiful daughter of yours?" Pierce asked. "Better to do the whole family in one go, don't you think?"

There was a distinct madness in Pierce's eyes. She had been so composed earlier, but it was clear now that something had shifted. The woman in front of her now was different, deranged.

"She's at the neighbor's," Matt answered too quickly. The guard tightened his grip.

Pierce raised her gun, pointing it at Rory.

"Why are you here?" Rory asked. "How did you even—"

There was a creaking noise behind her. She watched Matt's eyes flick to the area just behind her left arm.

"No," he whispered.

"Dad?" Sarah asked.

"*There* she is," Pierce said, her mad eyes finding Sarah behind Rory.

Pierce turned her gun toward Sarah. Instinctively, Rory stepped between the barrel and her daughter.

And then Matt made his move.

Rory watched him drive his elbow—with all his might—into the guard's groin. The guard screamed and released his hold. Pierce whirled around at the sound, and Rory turned, grabbed her daughter, and headed for the kitchen, swiping Matt's pistol off the countertop. She'd only ever shot it once, and she prayed that she remembered anything useful from that lesson.

She could hear a scuffle in the other room as she tucked Sarah into their pantry. It was decently hidden, a person had to push on the wood to get the door to pop out, and she knew it was her best bet. "Stay here," Rory said. "Don't move. I'll be right—" a single shot rang out, cutting off the rest of her sentence.

She spun around and ran back to the living room. Pierce was on top of Matt, blood pooled around them faster than Rory thought was possible. The guard was getting to his feet. Rory aimed and fired, and the guard dropped back to the floor, motionless.

In the scuffle, Pierce's gun had been knocked from her hand. She crawled over Matt to get it. Rory took aim at her outstretched palm and hoped for the best, firing. Pierce's index and middle fingers disappeared in a red blast and she *shrieked,* rolling off of Matt and raising her bloody hand to the sky.

That's when Rory saw that the blood pooling on her living room floor wasn't just from the other guard—most of it was her husband's.

She raced to his side as Pierce stood up and stumbled for the door. Rory raised Matt's pistol again, aimed one more shot, and fired. A red dot appeared in the calf of Pierce's white suit. She screamed again and pitched forward, but regained her balance and managed to get to the door. She half-dove through the doorframe and she was gone.

"Sarah," Matt said, eyes wild. "Is she okay?"

His face was white, but his voice was steady.

"She's okay," Rory said, her voice breaking. "Don't talk," Matt's stomach was a fountain of red. Rory put her hand over the hole and tried to stop the bleeding, but nothing helped. She couldn't wrap her head around how much blood was coming from such a small hole.

"Rory," Matt said. "Look at me."

She made herself.

"It's too late," he said. "It's okay. I'm not…" his voice faltered, his breath hitched as he tried to get the words out. "I'm not gonna make it."

Rory hadn't even noticed she was crying. This couldn't be happening. First Susan and the kids, and now Matt. He was her best friend, her companion, half of her heart and one of only two lights left in her darkening world. "Please…" she said, barely able to see through tears. "I can't do this without you."

He smiled, his lips blue now. "Yes you can," he said. "Take care of our daughter."

"Matt, please!" she sobbed. *This can't be happening.* "I can fix this. Just hold on, okay?" She looked around frantically as her husband's breathing slowed. "Somebody help me!" she screamed.

Matt's color was fading. He looked into Rory's eyes and, in that moment, everything was between them.

"Take care…of our daughter," he said again.

He took one final breath. Then his body seemed to sag, his eyes no longer focused, and Rory knew he was gone.

Please, God, help me. Please.

Her husband dead in her arms. Her, covered in his blood. His last words ringing in her ears.

Take care of our daughter.

2076

Now

Pierce

She does her best to clench and relax both of her hands and feet like she does every morning of this abysmal existence, making sure she can still feel her appendages. The cold has made her bad leg and hand so stiff that she has to make up her own physical therapy exercises each morning. Her limp worsens with every day, especially with the added mileage to keep pace with the boy and his party.

Pierce emerges from the tent and rolls her left ankle clockwise, then counterclockwise before starting her calf raises. The motions have gotten easier over time, but her leg never fully healed right and her left hand is useless. The world had descended into such chaos by the time she'd been shot, she hadn't been able to seek out proper medical care. One of her security guards had patched her up as best he could.

She always wakes before her two guards these days so she can have time to think. Today, like every other day, her father's enters her mind. Unwelcome, as always.

Jesus, Angela, Sergeant Major Pierce would have said to her now, *how fucking useless can you be?*

The old prick had died six years ago, just before she and

her team had been tasked with Operation Armageddon. Her father had built a pristine, cutthroat reputation during his time in the special forces and she'd followed him brilliantly. Armageddon should have been her most shining accomplishment to date.

But she'd underestimated the situation. Gravely. And now she was paying for it.

But she could still redeem herself. Those freak kids were the only chance they had left. That's why she had to catch up to the boy—he could lead her to the others. If not willingly, then forcefully. She couldn't stop now.

She'd made radio contact with what remained of the Armageddon staff after she'd come across the kids the first time. The others who had been left here to die. It was apparent none of them believed her, but she was able to get the information she needed.

She knew if she could bring the kids in and *show* her team what they were capable of, they could be studied. Dissected. Tested. Enhanced. Whatever it took to bring down the crits. It was unfortunate they'd lost the oldest one who seemed to be their leader, but no matter. From the strength they'd displayed, it was clear they'd only need a handful to defeat the crits.

The rest were expendable.

2072-2074

Then

Sarah

In the days after her father died, Sarah felt like the earth had shifted on its axis. She knew her mom tried to keep it together, but everything changed that day. Her mom had laughed and smiled all the time when her dad was around—even when things were shitty and getting shittier. But not after that.

Sarah went over every detail—over and over again—all the time. How, when she heard the fighting, she'd kicked open the pantry door, crawled out, and ran over to her mom's side, looking down at her dead father. How they'd both sat there in stunned silence for what seemed like hours, but was probably only minutes. How eventually she'd started to shake uncontrollably, which made her cry, which finally snapped her mom out of the daze she was in.

She'd watched as her mom's walls went up in real time. How she had wiped her face meticulously, finished packing their things, then called Sarah's grandparents and told them they'd meet at their family lake house just south of Denver.

But they never showed up.

For a while, they stayed at the lake house and planned. Her mom left during the day to gather supplies for an emergency, but they decided they'd ride it out until—if it came to it—they had to leave.

In the end, they did.

The lake house was tucked away in a beautiful, remote part of the state. They had no close neighbors which was a relief, and for a while Sarah thought they might be happy there.

She was wrong.

They'd made sure to lock and bolt the doors and windows every night. But one night, Sarah had been hot in her room, despite how cold it was getting outside, and she'd cracked the window just slightly to get some air. That's how he'd gotten in.

She awoke in the middle of the night to an enormous, calloused hand over her mouth. She smelled him before she could see him—he smelled like dirt and sweat, like he'd been outside for months.

Then she opened her eyes.

He had tiny beads of sweat clinging to his nose and his curly black beard. He wore a wool hat and a flannel shirt. But what she noticed most were his eyes. Those eyes had forgotten what it meant to be human. She felt something sharp press against the bottom of her chin.

"Scream and I'll cut your fucking thr—"

A shot tore through the quiet. His shoulder erupted. Sarah felt hard flecks of something land on her cheeks. Bone?

"FUCK!" he screamed, somehow still standing. He was the biggest man she'd ever seen. He whirled around and Sarah saw her mother pointing the barrel of a smoking rifle at him.

"Get the fuck out of my house," her mom said. Sarah thought, for a moment, about how calm her mother looked—except for her shaking hand.

"I like it when you girls play dirty," he responded, somehow *smiling* even though his shoulder was torn to shreds, and lunged at her.

Her mother backed up and pulled the trigger again, but there was a clicking sound Sarah knew from lessons with her dad—the gun was jammed.

"Shit," Rory said, her eyes finally betraying panic as she looked at Sarah. "*Run!*"

Sarah jumped up as the man moved for her mother with the knife. He brought it down, going for her eye, but Rory pushed it away at the last second and it plunged deep into her left cheek.

Sarah heard her mother shriek in agony.

"Run, Sarah!" she screamed.

Sarah ran. But not away.

She sprinted to the basement as fast as she could, taking the steps so quickly she nearly tripped and broke her neck. She knew her grandfather had a gun safe down here, and she knew it was stocked because they'd needed to take precautions when they arrived.

When she reached the safe, she could barely catch her breath. She fumbled with the lock, her tears coming so fast she could barely see. She could hear them upstairs—slamming against the floor and the walls. *Please don't let me be too late.*

When she finally got the safe open, she grabbed the first pistol she saw. Her dad used to take her out to shoot cans when things started to get bad, so she knew how to load and unload it. She did so with shaking hands, knowing every second mattered. Hoping her mother was still alive. Then she sprinted back upstairs.

Sarah got back to the bedroom to see the man straddling

her mother, his good hand on her throat, crushing her windpipe. Her mom's legs kicked out wildly beneath him, her hands useless to remove his tree trunk forearm. Sarah locked eyes with her mother for one moment, saw her mom's face torn open and gushing blood, and then raised the pistol and fired.

The shot rang out. A dark circle appeared in the middle of their attacker's forehead. *Bull's eye.*

Her mother gasped for air as he tumbled to the floor.

Sarah was thirteen years old.

2076

Now

Sarah

Sarah jolts awake. She has this dream often, always the same memory. Reliving it over and over again.

She looks around, and it's dark. Always dark. She shivers in her sleeping bag and wonders how it's possible to survive a cold any worse than this. And the further north they trek, the colder it will get.

In the last few weeks, they've made their way through Utah and into Idaho. They have just over a month until they reach Calgary.

If they reach Calgary.

The cold is their biggest enemy. It drains them all faster than ever, and since they have to ration their food, they hardly have any energy left at the end of the day to train. But still, they do it every night. Sarah will never forget what those lessons had given her in the moment she needed them most. And neither, she knew, would Sam. But now, a new purpose drives her through the training.

. . .

Even though Sam has been able to get a few small animals for them, the hunting is terrible. Everything is dead, it seems, except for the four of them. Hunger, cold, and darkness are their constant companions. But still, what keeps Sarah putting one foot in front of the other is the thought of Pierce. Over the last few weeks, since Sam told them about the "cold woman," Pierce is all she can think about. The memories came back slowly, but they came back. Every minute of every day she thinks about killing Pierce—and it scares her. She remembers the way she'd smiled at them, all those years ago. She remembers seeing her father's body in a pool of blood. And she remembers, mostly, what it felt like to kill that man who had tried to kill her mother. And she hates to admit it, but in that moment—watching him topple to the ground—it had felt good.

She rises early—as she has every day since Sam told them about Pierce—and sneaks quietly out of the tent. Her eyesight is the best of the group, and she wants to—for once in her life—use it to become the hunter.

She knows her mother will never approve of what she's doing, but she can't help herself. Each morning when she wakes now, she retraces their steps a mile or so from the day before. Sarah knows Pierce will never give up on finding Jacob—or maybe, she just hopes it.

But if her plan works, she'll be the one to find Pierce first.

2076

Now

RORY

IDAHO CAME AND WENT WITHOUT INCIDENT. But after what Sam told them the other night, Rory can't shake the feeling that they are being tracked. And she studies Jacob constantly—the boy who says almost nothing, but who has become their most valuable asset.

"He can't always control it," Sam says to her one day as they walk, somewhere near Missoula, Montana.

"Control what?" Rory asks.

"Jacob. I've seen him, I don't know, lose it a few times or something."

Rory has been wondering about this since that night in Moab. They'd been surrounded, and Jacob hadn't been able to help them. As she looks ahead to see him smiling up at Sarah, she sees what she always sees. He's just a child. Of course he can't control it.

"He's just a kid, Sam," Rory says. "He probably can't even understand what it is. He has no idea what it means. He's afraid, just like the rest of us."

Sam sighs. "That's exactly what I thought, too," he says. "I just want him to be normal. To have a normal life. To be a *kid.*"

"That's all I've ever wanted for Sarah," Rory says. "But sadly, this is the world they got," she gestures around to the frozen, moonlit grayscape.

"Maybe," Sam says. "Or maybe not. Maybe this place in Calgary is legit, who knows? Maybe they can make friends, and tell stories, and laugh again."

Rory wants to believe it, too. "You've never really given up, have you?"

Sam smiles at her. "I've been very close," he says. "After Becca…I could barely keep moving. But really, it was Jacob that saved me. The last thing she asked me to do was to take care of him—to get him to Calgary. And I plan to."

Take care of our daughter.

"I definitely understand that," Rory says.

"You've seen what that kid can do," Sam says, looking at her. "Are you ready to give up yet?"

He's right, she knows. She's felt a change in herself since they'd met Sam and Jacob. They've made it so far—through so much—and they are so close now. Finally, she has a flicker of hope for what's to come.

. . .

As they make their way through Montana, Rory can't help but take in the scenery. Even in the dark, it's some of the most beautiful country she has ever seen. And in complete desolation, it really feels like the last frontier. One day, a bear cub crosses their path. Sam grabs the back of Sarah's pack and pulls her backward, slowly. Rory reaches for Jacob's hand and does the same. She feels all the hair on her body stand on end—the mother bear has to be close behind.

And she is.

They hear the branches snapping under her before she emerges, but when she does, Rory's heart sinks. The mother bear is skeletal. Rory has no idea how she's still moving.

The mother bear stops, turns, and looks directly at Rory. She lets out a plume of steamy breath from her snout. And that's when Rory realizes it: her and this bear are the same. Two mothers in the middle of the end of the fucking world with their cubs. They keep moving for the same reason.

Because they have to.

. . .

A few days after the bear, they reach Glacier National Park—its enormous, pointed mountains standing silently over what's left of the American west. They camp at Lake McDonald under a full moon. All four of them, despite the bitter cold, sit on the edge of the lake in total silence. The water has become a black sheet of ice that reflects the stars so perfectly, it looks like there are two skies: one above them and one at their feet. Rory would always remember it as one of the best nights of her life. Later, she'd wonder—if she'd known what was coming, would she have done anything differently? Would she have held onto those moments a little tighter? Would she have told them all how much they meant to her?

The what ifs are endless. The reality is that, in life, all we can do is our best with the hand we're dealt.

2076

Now

SARAH

A FEW DAYS AFTER GLACIER, they camp in a town called Diamond Valley. Sarah rises early as usual and silently sneaks away from the tent. They are only a day from Calgary now. She's desperate to find Pierce before they run out of time. Or worse, if Pierce *is* still following them, they'll lead her right to the safe house.

She walks about a mile and a half in the direction they came from yesterday when she spots a tent about 100 yards from her. Her heart stops. *Please,* she thinks. *Let me be right about this.*

She creeps toward the tent as quietly as possible. Are they inside? She'd imagined that they would be, but she realizes she hasn't thought about what she'd do if they aren't. She hasn't thought much about this plan at all, in fact. She'd thought through finding Pierce, sure, but then what?

Whatever happens, though, she knows she can handle it. She's been training. She's ready.

When she's about twenty yards from the tent, afraid to even breathe too loudly, she sees a dash of white-blond hair.

Got you, she thinks, unholstering her weapon and staying tight to the tree line.

Pierce is walking into the woods, it looks like, for a bathroom trip.

Sarah smiles.

She tracks Pierce through the trees. Watching. Waiting.

Pierce finally stops next to a dead oak and reaches for the zipper on her pants.

Sarah kicks off the safety.

"And to think, I could have caught you with your pants down," Sarah says, pleased with herself for thinking of that line on the spot.

Pierce doesn't even seem surprised. She turns slowly, and raises her hands. For some reason, she's smiling.

Sarah stares at her. After days of scouting, she has Pierce exactly where she wants her. Looking at her now with her limp and her missing fingers, all the memories come flooding back with a force that nearly brings her to her knees. But she can't falter. Not now.

"Do you remember me?" Sarah asks.

Pierce shrugs. "Should I?" she says.

"You killed my father," Sarah says. "The day everything went to shit. You ruined my family. You ruined hundreds of families."

Pierce says nothing.

All she has to do, Sarah knows, is pull the trigger. And yet, she can't. *Why?*

"You know, I've thought about what I'd say to you," Pierce says, smiling. "Maybe try convincing you to help us save the world—I've seen you traveling with that little boy."

What does that mean? Sarah thinks. But she says, "I would never help you in a million fucking years."

Pierce's blue eyes dart into the distance somewhere just over Sarah's right shoulder. A twig snaps.

"Oh," Pierce says. "But you already are."

Sarah feels cold steel press into the back of her head.

"Drop your gun or I'll blow your skull open," says a deep voice behind her.

Shit.

2076

Now

Rory

WHEN SHE WAKES UP, Sarah isn't next to her in the tent. This used to scare her when Sarah was younger, but now she knows not to worry. She's probably just outside relieving herself. Rory snags her wool hat and thick winter coat before tugging on her boots to step outside into the cold darkness of Diamond Valley.

The stars are endless. The last few years without electricity have erased all the light pollution, giving them an unobstructed view. Galaxies she'd never seen before weave together across the sky above the Canadian Rocky Mountains. Rory thinks, for a moment, about the power of nature. Dinosaurs extinct, ice ages, and now total darkness have all come to pass—millennia over millennia—and still, the natural world soldiered on.

Would humans?

She looks around and realizes Sarah is nowhere in sight. Only then does she begin to panic.

. . .

Rory tears the tent zipper down and crawls back inside, shaking Sam awake.

"Sam!" she says, grabbing his shoulders. "Sam, wake up!"

His eyes snap open. Instinctively, he grabs his gun. "What is it?" he says.

"Sarah's gone," Rory says, heart hammering, trying to get her breathing under control.

"Okay," he says. "It's going to be okay. Did she say anything at all about leaving?"

"Nothing," Rory says. "How about to you, Jacob?"

The boy shakes his head, looking frightened.

Rory racks her brain—*think*. Where could she have possibly gone?

"She's been acting strange since the other night," Rory says slowly. "Since you told us about Pierce. You don't think..." she trails off. Sam is eyeing her.

"I don't think, what?" he asks.

"You don't think she would've gone looking for them, do you?" she asks quietly. *Please don't let her be that stupid.*

Sam is already mostly dressed as he pulls his boots on, tucks his pistol into the back of his pants, and grabs his rifle. "I don't know, but if she did, she probably thinks they're tracking us," he said. "I'll retrace our steps from yesterday."

"Hang on, I'm coming with you," Rory says.

Sam kneels down and puts a calming hand on her shoulder. "Someone needs to be here if she comes back, and we can't leave Jacob alone. This is what I used to do," he says, giving her shoulder a squeeze. "I'll find her."

Sam turns to Jacob. "Do everything Rory tells you to do, okay? I'll be back soon." He kisses the boy on the cheek and ducks out of the tent.

Rory sits with her head in her hands. She hates being fucking useless. Why did she have to bring up those memories of Pierce? If Sarah *was* really out there and something happened…she can't even finish the thought.

A little hand reaches out and squeezes her forearm. Rory looks up.

"It's going to be okay," Jacob says quietly.

She smiles, wiping a tear away. "Thank you," she says.

And so they wait.

2076

Now

SAM

SAM HAD DONE HIS SHARE OF TRACKING when he was in the army. Luckily, Sarah's boots have left the slightest impression over the frosted earth, and he follows the footprints to the tree line. It is extremely difficult to look for signs of her in the dark, but sporadic use of his flashlight shows broken spider-webs along a trail where, he hopes, she walked through not long before him.

He kicks himself the entire way, knowing that he'd likely inspired this bout of heroism, if that's what Sarah's going for. The training, he would never regret. But he should've been smarter—he should've told her that you don't go looking for a fight. You only stand your ground when the fight finds you.

If anything happens to her, he knows he'll never forgive himself. But he can't let his mind go there—not yet, at least. He's lost too much already. So he keeps his head down, and he follows as many of the footprints as he can see in the darkness of the forest.

After about a mile, when he's mostly lost her steps and is going on his compass and instinct, he hears voices. They're distant, but approaching quickly.

"Get off me!" Sarah shouts. His heart sinks. *Fuck.*

"Do shut *up*," a cold, familiar voice answers. "That scream-ing will attract every crit within 100 miles."

"Good!" Sarah shouts. "Then something will finally kill you."

"Gag her," is all he hears Pierce say, just as they make their way into Sam's line of sight.

He flattens himself against a tree, breathes slowly, and watches. He sees Pierce and her two men, and in one of their arms is Sarah. His mind races to calculate his next move. If he attacks from here, it's likely that Sarah would be killed or he'd be taken down before he could do much damage. He has to bide his time.

"This doesn't end well for you if you don't help us, you know," Pierce says to Sarah, who is thrashing against the enormous hands of one of Pierce's henchmen. "You hand over the boy, or you all die and we take him anyway."

"Uck…oo!" Sarah garbles against the gag tied around her mouth.

"Suit yourself," says Pierce. "But do you really think he's the only one of his kind? Do you have any idea what we could do with an army of them?"

Others? Sam's mind races.

"You didn't know?" Pierce says.

Sarah scowls back at Pierce, but it's clear that she's just as shocked as Sam.

"I came across a group of them about a year ago some-where in Missouri." Pierce says. "We were just walking aim-lessly back then, wondering every day if we should just give up, when we saw them. They were so young, and they were making so much noise, I knew it would attract something. And it did," she paused. "We heard that fucking terrible noise and ducked behind a building. Then we waited. Sure enough, it came running for them. I figured it would kill all of them in a matter of seconds, but I watched them all put their hands up. At first I had no idea what to make of it, but then I saw what it *did*."

She turns to Sarah. "They are so powerful. We could open them up, study them, enhance their skills. Maybe even defeat the crits in just a matter of days."

So Sam had been right. Jacob was nothing more than a lab rat to this woman. And there were others. Did Jacob have siblings?

Sam stays tucked behind a tree and watches them go. He trails behind them in the forest, thinking fast.

Regardless of the revelation Pierce has just dumped on them, one thing is certain: He has to save his kids.

2076

Now

RORY

HER PANIC CRESCENDOES while she waits with Jacob at the tent for Sam and Sarah to get back. For twenty minutes after Sam left, Rory got up and paced back and forth outside the tent, looking up every few minutes to see if Sarah was walking back, saying something like "Sorry! I went to explore the area…" not even realizing how worried she'd made them all.

That hadn't happened. It was now past 8 a.m.. Sarah never would have left for this long without saying anything.

Rory sits in the tent with her head between her legs, breathing steadily to try and calm her heart rate, hating how completely helpless she feels. Her mind is at war with itself.

I should've gone and had Sam stay here, she thinks one minute. *He's more likely to find her than you and you know it,* she thinks the next. Anxiety threatens to turn her guts inside out. She breathes slowly, intentionally, in and out.

He's going to find her, she tells herself over and over. *He's going to find her.*

But then she hears another voice.

Take care of our daughter.

She sees his face as he takes his last breath. His last—and only—command of her in their life together.

What has she done?

That's when she feels a tiny form crawl across the tent and snuggle into her side. Jacob lays a small hand on her arm and squeezes.

"It's going to be okay," he whispers again.

She almost laughs at the absurdity of it—the sunlight is gone, the world is overrun by monsters, and she's lost her daughter. Is any of it okay?

But she looks down at him, wipes her eyes, and squeezes his arm back.

"Thank you," she says. And he smiles.

Then they hear footsteps approaching outside.

. . .

Four dark figures traipse across the valley. Rory recognizes the outline of her daughter immediately. She'd recognize her anywhere, at any distance, even squinting through the darkness. She sees another small figure in the front with a pronounced limp in her right leg.

Pierce.

Her heartbeat accelerates, but she takes a steadying breath. The time for fear is over.

Rory tucks a pistol into her waistband and out of sight. She tells Jacob to stay put before she steps outside.

Her daughter stands in the clutches of one of Pierce's men, gagged, with a knife at her throat. The sight nearly brings Rory to her knees, but she has one shot at getting this right.

Take care of our daughter.

"We wondered where she'd wandered off to," Rory says across the distance between them, her voice betraying no fear. "Thanks for returning her to us…unharmed."

Pierce smiles. The same smile Rory remembers from that other lifetime. Empty. Soulless. Damned.

"Where is the boy?" Pierce says.

"What boy?" answers Rory.

The man who holds Sarah tightens his grip, thrusting the knife even closer to her throat now. Close enough to draw blood. Here they are again.

Stay calm.

Pierce smiles. "Let me simplify this," she says. "You give us the boy and your daughter lives."

Rory's heart sinks.

"No!" Although Sarah's cry is muffled, Rory hears it loud and clear.

"If you don't shut *up,*" Pierce says, "I'm going to tell him to—ah," she sighs, looking up. "*There* he is."

Rory hadn't heard anything, but when she looks down to her right, Jacob is there next to her, shaking like a leaf.

"No!" Sarah bites out again through the gag.

Pierce doesn't hear her this time. She has one focus. "Now, it's quite simple. Give him to us. Or watch my man slit your daughter's throat."

Rory's mind works fast. "Wait—" she starts.

Pierce spits out a laugh. "Trust me," she takes a step forward. "I have waited long enough. Jackson!" she turns to her man, "I think she needs some convincing."

"WAIT!" Rory yells.

A shot rings out behind them. Rory leaps nearly a foot off the ground at the sound. Then the man holding Sarah crumples, a pool of red forming around his head.

Sarah doesn't waste a second. The other man lunges for her, but she plants her feet and uses all of her force to drive the heel of her palm into his nose, which spurts blood with a satisfying *snap* that even Rory can hear from where she's standing. Then she sets off at a run toward Rory and Jacob, just as Rory sees Pierce lift a pistol, targeting her daughter's back.

"No!" Rory and Jacob say at once.

But Jacob's palms are already raised toward Pierce, who—along with her bleeding crony—are thrown backward nearly ten yards, landing in a tangled pile on the frozen ground.

Rory snatches her rifle from outside the tent, tosses her pistol to Sarah, and grabs Jacob's hand as she runs all of them for cover in the nearby treeline. She spots Sam to her right as they all duck behind a stand of cedars—his rifle raised and still aimed toward Pierce.

"Thank you," she breathes when she sees him.

"Are you hurt?" he asks.

"We're okay," she answers. She looks at her daughter who is removing the gag from her mouth with violently shaking hands. Jacob sits in between them, clinging to Rory's coat.

Are they okay?

Sam dares a step out from behind his tree to look, and another shot pierces the air. Rory hears the *thunk* as it hits somewhere nearby. Sam fires back.

"Got him," Sam says.

Rory looks around just in time to see the last henchmen collapse and Pierce sprint for cover behind a boulder a few feet from their tent.

"You're all fools!" Pierce shrieks. "That boy is the future!" Rory can hear the same hysteria she'd heard all those years ago.

"What about Mars, Pierce?" Rory yells back, stalling. "Ships left without you?"

Silence.

Rory nearly laughs. "You really don't remember us?" she asks.

Silence again, this time for so long Rory figures Pierce won't respond.

"Oh, I remember you," Pierce finally says. "Colorado. You and your stupid friend, Nick Fischer. Thorn in my fucking side. He's dead, by the way."

The jab lands. Rory had always suspected, but knowing for sure doesn't make it any easier.

"He ruined my shot at getting on a ship," she says. "So perhaps I should be thanking him."

What?

Rory turns to look at Sarah, but her daughter has crept away. She now stands huddled behind a tree a few yards away, pistol aimed at Pierce, just beyond Pierce's line of sight.

Rory nearly cries out. What is she doing?

"What are you talking about?" Rory asks, trying to distract Pierce. "Why would you thank him for that?"

Pierce sighs. Heavy, unabashed exhaustion. "None of it matters anymore," she says. "Just give me the boy, and I'll go away forever. I'll stop hunting you."

"You're the one being hunted, bitch," Sarah says, stepping out from behind the tree.

Pierce turns at the sound, raising her pistol at Sarah.

A single shot tears through the darkness.

"Sarah!" Rory shouts. Coverage be damned, she leaps to her feet and charges through the trees toward her daughter. Her mind flashes to another time. Another place. A carpet stained with blood. Matt's eyes, open but unseeing.

Take care of our daughter.

But there Sarah stands. Upright and unharmed.

It is Pierce who has fallen. Her crouched body has slid out from behind the rock she'd been cowering behind, dark red blood staining the gray earth.

Sarah's eyesight had given her the advantage over them all.

Rory and Sarah approach Pierce together, who crawls pathetically toward her gun. Rory kicks it out of reach, and Pierce finally turns onto her back, looking at them.

"Your father," Pierce wheezes. Sarah's shot has surely collapsed a lung. "Did he die?"

"Fuck you," Sarah says, raising her pistol.

Rory puts her hand over her daughter's.

"Sarah," she whispers, putting a finger under her daughter's chin and turning her, so that they face one another. She looks her daughter in the eye. "You know who you are. Don't let her take that away from you." Rory reaches for the gun.

Sarah's hands shake. Her eyes fill with tears.

"She killed him," Sarah whispers. "She ruined everything, and I still can't finish her."

"Because you don't want to become her," Rory says. "I know you're angry. I am, too. But don't do this. Let go."

Sarah releases the pistol and nods. She turns away from them, walking back to join Sam and Jacob, who look on just out of earshot.

Rory stares down at the woman who has taken everything from her. How many times has she imagined this moment? And yet, she feels nothing.

"Tell me what you meant back there," Rory says. "That you should thank Nick Fischer."

Even inches from death, Pierce smiles. "The ships," she says, wincing in pain as she draws in a breath "nearly all of them were taken by the mobs…or they waited too long and the crits took them. Only one made it out." Blood spills out the side of her mouth. "We heard from them, a few months later. The crits had already made it to Mars. It was too late."

"You're lying," Rory says.

Pierce smiles, one last, horrible time. "Why would I? It's over for me now, too. That broadcast—the ships they mentioned. None of it matters." She laughs, a wet, sloppy sound. Her eyes close. "Your only chance now is that boy, and the others. And you're all too stupid to see it."

"Others?" Rory says. "What do you mean, others?"

But it's too late. From across the clearing, Rory hears a chittering. The shooting had made too much noise.

She turns and jogs back to the treeline with the others.

"Wait!" Pierce yells, her eyes at last betraying fear. "Don't leave me here!"

Rory smiles as she ducks for cover behind a tree, just as the crit finds Pierce.

2076

Now

Sam

He'd been hit. Sometime in the shootout with Pierce, a bullet had gone in one side of his shoulder and out the other. Thankfully it didn't puncture the lung, and he can't tell how bad it is, but he's losing a lot of blood. He's sure of that.

They are a day from Calgary. They are also on the precipice of the new moon. Total darkness will arrive in a few short hours, meaning they'll have to wait at this camp site for two more nights. He doesn't have to do the math to know what that means: he'll be dead before they reach Calgary.

The universe's last joke at his expense.

He taps Rory on the shoulder outside the tent while they prepare to hunker down and wait out the new moon.

"I need to talk to you," he says.

She nods, and they walk down to the lake.

There is no point in lying or making this harder than it needs to be. He opens his jacket, despite the freezing cold, exposing the bullet wound in his shoulder.

Rory closes her eyes, lowers her head. "We need to bandage that up," she says.

"We will," Sam says. "But I won't last the next two nights

here, and we both know it. I'm going to die in that tent, and I need to know, without a doubt, that you'll get them to the safe house."

She nods. "I will." There's something off. She won't meet his eyes.

"What is it?" Sam asks.

"It's nothing," she says.

"Rory. Tell me."

She sighs. "Pierce told me that the ships are bullshit. That the crits have already made it to Mars. That this broadcast, even if this safe house *does* exist, it's not an offer for a new life. Not really, anyway."

His heart sinks. They'd come all this way for nothing.

"For fuck's sake," he says.

"Maybe she was lying," Rory says. "But…"

"But why would she?" Sam finishes.

"Exactly."

"So we have two bad options," Sam says, the pain in his shoulder a constant, dull throbbing. "I die before we can move, and you take the kids alone to the safe house to see if it really *is* a safehouse or if it's a trap. And if it's a trap, you all die."

Rory winces.

"Or," Sam says, hesitating for a moment. "When I die, you guys make your way south as far as you can go and maybe it gets warmer. And you try to keep them alive."

Rory looks away. He can see how tired she is. She and Sarah had started out by going south, and now he's asking them to go all the way back?

"Or," Sarah says from behind them, "we go tonight."

"God damn it, Sarah—" Rory starts.

"We heard you. We hear everything," her eyes are wet.

"We're not losing any more people, okay?" She walks over and looks Sam in the eyes. "You're going to make it, do you understand?"

He smiles. "Okay," he says, hoping it's not a lie.

"The new moon starts tonight," Rory says. "It's too dangerous."

"Jesus, Mom," Sarah says. "Look around. It's never *not* dangerous. We're a day out. We can travel light, just take the emergency bags." She looks at them, defiance in her eyes. Just like her father. "We all make it, or we all die."

"You're not allowed to die," a little voice says. "None of you."

Sam looks down and sees Jacob walking over to them, green eyes bright as ever.

"Understood, kid," Sam says.

Rory sighs and takes a few steps away from them. Sam can see exhaustion etched in every line of her face. She stares up at the sky, as if she's hoping for an answer. Then she turns back around.

"Okay," she says, putting a hand on her daughter's shoulder "We're not losing anybody else."

They stand in silence, looking around at each other with something Sam was certain at one point he'd never feel again: love.

Then Rory clears her throat. "If we're going to do this, you need to do every single thing that we tell you to do, understood?" she says, looking at Jacob and Sarah. "Every. Single. Thing. No matter how hard it is or how much you don't want to do it. Okay?"

They both nod.

"Even if that means leaving us to save yourselves," Rory finishes.

"Mom—" Sarah starts.

"This is not a negotiation," Rory says firmly. "It's a yes, or we don't go."

Sarah and Jacob look at each other and then nod again.

"Okay," she says, turning to Sam. "First, let's get that shoulder bandaged.

They patch up Sam's shoulder as well as they can with their medical supplies from Moab. But the bleeding is ceaseless, and he knows the bandage is a short-term fix. They have to move quickly. He's on borrowed time now. And for the first time in a long time, he wants to *live*.

The moon disappears in the hours they prepare to leave, unpacking whatever they don't need as quickly and quietly as they can. And all the while, Sam feels his strength wane. This, he knows, is his final stretch.

As long as he gets his newfound family safely to Calgary, he will embrace whatever is in store for himself.

They set out with Sarah at the front of the group. If anything moves up ahead, or if there are traps laid at the outskirts of town, her eyes are the best and she can signal to the rest of them. The darkness is suffocating. But even with no moon, and even through the dense, deep dark, what Sam can see of the landscape takes his breath away. The Canadian Rockies tower over a wide, open terrain that stretches for miles in every direction. Even before the darkness took over, Sam knew that this land had been largely unspoiled by mankind. It makes him smile to see that at least this small, perfect patch of the world has remained.

He can imagine what it was like here before—an entire midwestern community. Families with children just trying to get by in a world of constant sunlight. What had it looked like when the darkness started closing in? Had they known about the safe house? Were the empty houses only abandoned because people had gone there, and were safely waiting for others to arrive?

He hoped so. He hoped they'd get somewhere that Sarah and Jacob could make friends. Where they could be kids and laugh and not worry about defending themselves against the monsters among them now.

He hoped.

And while he hoped, they kept walking. And while they walked, his shoulder kept bleeding.

2076

Now

Sarah

She and her mother had almost never been outside the tent during the new moon other than to go to the bathroom. They'd certainly never walked during it. But now, there is no other choice. At least not one that involves Sam surviving the journey, which is non-negotiable.

They walk single-file. Four tiny ants on a star-washed, mountain-studded canvas. Sarah is entirely alone with her thoughts as they stretch across everything from her father to that horrible night at the lake house to her final look at Pierce.

She can see her breath clearly against the darkness. Her face is so cold. She can feel tiny icicles on her eyelashes. But still, she knows they have to trudge on. The anger she'd tended to like a fire for so long, her anger at losing her father, at Pierce, at this cold, shitty world, has finally been replaced by something else: hope. Hope for a new journey in Calgary. Hope for friendships with people she hasn't met yet. Hope for the safety of her new family.

Behind her, she hears a rustling sound and a thud. She whips around in an instant, unholstering her gun and preparing to fight back. But there is only the *pat pat pat* of Jacob's boots on the hard ground as he runs to Sam, who has fallen to his knees.

Sarah and her mom reach him at the same time.

"Sam," Sarah dares to whisper, putting a hand on his shoulder. "Are you okay?"

"Yes," he says. "But I think…I may need some help the rest of the way."

Sarah sees movement to her left and whips her head around, raising her pistol. But it's just a scrawny, desperate squirrel searching the land for something—anything—to eat.

"Lean on me, Sam," her mom says. "Jacob, you walk ahead of us with Sarah."

Jacob nods, and Sarah takes his hand. Her mother heaves Sam to his feet and he grimaces in agony.

Her mom tosses Sam's good arm around her shoulders, supporting most of his weight. "Okay?" she asks.

Sam nods.

So they walk on.

. . .

Their pace has slowed significantly with Sam leaning on her mom. Every hour or so, they have to sit down and take a break. And with every hour, Sam's skin gets grayer.

"We need to check your bandage," her mom whispers when they stop around midnight. Sarah's eyes strain into the treeline. Her ears listening for the tiniest sound.

When her mom reaches for the zipper on his jacket, her hand comes away bloody. Sarah watches as her mother pulls Sam's jacket down just enough to expose his shoulder. The pristine white bandage they'd applied this morning is soaked in red.

"We need to change this," her mom says.

Though his under eyes are heavy with dark circles, Sam looks at her resolutely. "There's no time," he says. "Too much noise. We need to keep moving."

"Sam—" her mom starts.

"Let's go," he says.

Sarah nods, patting Jacob on the head. "He'll be okay," she whispers to him.

But she knows even as she says it, she is trying to convince herself too.

2076

Now

Rory

After three hours of creeping through the dying spruce trees, they reach the Calgary city limits. Sam is nearly a head taller than Rory and outweighs her by at least fifty pounds, and her knees threaten to buckle under the strain. Her jacket is soaked with the blood that now covers Sam's entire torso. She can smell it against her face as he leans on her, coppery and warm. Her toes are freezing, and her teeth are so cold it hurts to breathe through her mouth. She's never felt cold like this—this deep in her bones. Every so often she flexes her fingers inside her mitten, just to make sure she still can. But on the hand she's using to support Sam, she can no longer feel her pinky finger at all. Fatigue has become a part of her over the years, embedding itself into her skin. But she's never felt this tired before. Her legs are like cement. But she has to keep going.

"So...cold," Sam breathes, a plume of steam coming from his mouth.

"I know," Rory says. "We're almost there."

Though they'd passed through the outskirts of many cities on their journey north, Rory still finds it eerie as hell. The silhouette of Calgary's skyline stands out against the stars in the distance. The mountain peaks open up to make room for the city, and yet there is utter silence. No city lights to guide them the rest of the way. No traffic. No sign of life whatsoever except for the sound of four pairs of desperate footsteps, padding across the earth.

Sam sags slightly, and she hoists him up back onto her shoulder.

One step at a time, she thinks.

Then he sags again, only this time she can't keep her grip. He falls to the earth. The sound tears through the seams of the silence around them. Her heart races, and she strains her ears for any indication that they'd been heard. But all she hears is silence.

"Come on, Sam," she whispers. "Get up."

"Can't," he says, breathing heavily. "You go. I'll die."

"No," says Jacob, who'd approached silently. "Get up." He holds his hand out, palm facing the sky, as if to give Sam a hand. Instead, as Jacob raises his palm, Sam's body begins to rise.

"Get up," says Jacob again, gently. "Please."

Sam's body rises slowly, his face twisted in excruciation. Rory reaches out to support him as he gets higher and higher until he is, once again, on his feet, leaning against her. His face is covered in a thin layer of sweat, which makes her realize she's sweating too. She doesn't know how long she can carry him. She is so tired.

"Not allowed to die," Jacob whispers again.

Rory turns her head to look at Sam. Even through his pain, he's smiling.

"Okay, Jacob," he says.

Sam looks down at Rory and nods. "I'm ready," he says. "Let's keep going."

She nods back, hoists him up higher on her shoulder, and trudges on.

. . .

They make it another fifteen minutes when the forest starts to retreat and the land grows flat and clear around them. Rory doesn't like the exposure, but she knows it means they're getting closer to the city. They pass a gas station where she imagines commuters had refueled every day on their way home from work. Abandoned cars begin to appear in the parking lots of the rundown stores around them. She sees that Sarah has stopped ahead and is pointing at something. It had once been a highway sign, but now it reads something else.

Safe house 1 mile. Food. Water. Shelter.

Rory dares to hope. *Is it real?*

"Sam," she says. "Look."

Sam's head lolls forward, and it seems to take all of his strength to look up at the sign.

"We're going to make it," Rory says.

Every few yards, there are more.

Three-quarters of a mile.

Half a mile.

It's when they get to the quarter of a mile sign that Sarah freezes up ahead, raising her right hand. The signal for them all to stop.

Rory's heart plummets. *Not now. Please.*

They are so close. What can her daughter see that she can't?

And then she hears it.

From a distance, that chittering noise begins. But as she listens, the sound seems to grow.

There's more than one.

Has this been a trap all along?

But then she looks down and sees that Sam's blood covers her boots. She turns her head and can just make out the glistening patches of blood in their wake.

They've left a perfect trail for the crits to follow.

Up ahead, Sarah turns to them so slowly, it's like she's moving through molasses. Her eyes are huge as she stares at something behind them.

Rory turns, as gently as she can, to see whatever it is.

A flurry of motion against the darkness. The sound is getting louder.

She snaps her head back around and locks eyes with her daughter.

"Run," Rory whispers.

Sarah grabs Jacob's hand and they take off at a sprint.

"Come on, Sam," Rory says. "We have to move." Had they made it this far just to die here at the final stretch?

She starts to run, but Sam is so heavy against her. She's half dragging him as his weight crushes her.

"Come on!" she yells, no point in whispering now. "Whatever you have left, Sam, I need you to use it right now!"

They push on, together, making it one yard at a time, Sam stumbling and Rory catching him. When she dares to look up, she can see a building in the distance. The safe house? She hopes it's true. But still, it's too far. Just barely out of reach. The sound around her escalates, that horrible chittering coming from all directions now.

She looks over at Sam, who is nearly unconscious standing up. They'll never make it, and it hits her like an oncoming truck: she is going to die.

She chokes on a sob. *The kids will make it,* she thinks. And really, that's all that matters.

Next to her, she feels Sam start to slip. She tries to hold him up, tries to keep dragging his immobile feet, but she can't. He collapses, one last time.

"No!" she cries. "Please, Sam. Get *up!*"

"Take care of them," he says. And she can't believe she's here again. The same tragedy. The same words. A different lifetime.

"Don't you fucking say that," she says. "Get UP!" Every time she tries to lift him, he slips. Her body is exhausted from fielding his weight all day. Her arms are rubber. She can't lift him.

The sound is all around them now. Rory can hear the spider-like legs thundering across the frozen tundra toward them.

"You have to leave me," Sam whispers. "I can buy you some time."

"No," Rory says, voice shaking. She grabs his jacket, trying to drag him if she can't carry him, but he cries out in agony. "Get the fuck up, Sam."

She heaves with all her strength to get him upright, screaming with the effort. She manages to lift him a foot off the ground, only for him to crash down again. He is dead weight.

Sam's eyes open and close. Open and close. "Go," he says. His eyes shut one last time.

"Sam!" she hears her daughter shout.

No. Please, God, no.

"What the hell are you doing here?" Rory screams as she sees Sarah and Jacob sprinting back to join her. "Get to the safe house!"

A crit screeches out of the darkness, barreling at them full-tilt. Sarah screams.

Jacob steps in front of them, one arm extended toward the crit. It is blasted back nearly thirty yards.

Rory has made her choice—the only choice. She rests Sam's head on the ground. "I'm sorry Sam," she whispers. "I'm so sorry."

Then she turns to Sarah and Jacob. "We need to go," she shouts. "*Now.*"

"We're not leaving him!" Sarah screams, wiping her eyes.

Another crit charges at them, and Jacob blasts it back again.

"What did I say before?" Rory yells back. "Listen to every single thing I tell you. Let's go!"

Just then, another sound joins the shrieking crits. A rumbling. An engine?

Headlights pierce the darkness, blinding all of them. The light illuminates Sam's face and Rory gasps in horror. He has lost so much blood. His skin is gray, his eyes are shut. But she can just make out the steam around his nose. He is breathing, but barely.

Another screech comes from the darkness, and Jacob sends another crit flying, yelling with the effort. But Rory can see the toll it takes on him. His face is drenched in sweat, dark circles appearing around his eyes.

A Jeep bears down on them and, for a moment, Rory thinks the driver is planning to run them all over. But the car skids to a stop a few feet from them, sending frozen dirt flying into their faces.

The driver's side door flies open. "Get in!" a man's voice shouts.

"Go!" Rory yells at Sarah and Jacob, who leap inside the Jeep.

"I can't move him," Rory says. "Please, help me!"

The man leaps out. A white beard covers his face under a wool hat. He runs over to her.

"Oh my God," he breathes. "Sam?"

There is no time to think about it. "Help me get him up!" Rory screams. The man grabs Sam under his arms and heaves. Sam groans, but his eyes stay shut. The man is strong, moving Sam easily to the Jeep.

Is this really happening? She grabs Sam's legs and helps the stranger lift him into the back seat with the kids.

"Jacob!" the man yells. "Oh my God. Is it really you?"

"We don't have time for this!" Rory yells. "Get *in!*"

The man jumps back into the driver's seat and Rory runs around to the passenger's side. She hasn't even closed her door when he jams on the accelerator, kicking up more frozen ground behind them. In the rearview, Rory can see a wall of crits closing in on them. They have no choice. They have to trust him.

"Hold on!" the man shouts as they approach the safe house. One-hundred yards, fifty yards, twenty yards. A garage door opens ahead of them, where another man stands, arms windmilling frantically to wave them in.

An explosion erupts behind them. For one beautiful second, the entire world lights up. Rory has a flash-memory of living in sunlight. Ahead of them, she can see the enormous safe house, and she realizes it's an old shopping mall. She sees the driver's face in full. He looks exhausted, but kind. He has laugh lines around his eyes and white hair peeking out from beneath his hat.

Though her heart is racing, exhaustion threatens to pull her under. The Jeep lurches forward from the force of the explosion behind them, and then she hears the sound. The crits screaming behind her, gargling and crying in pain.

They cross the threshold of the garage and a heavy door closes behind them, plunging them once again into darkness.

A light flickers on overhead.

"Did we make it?" she asks the man driving the car.

"You made it," he says. "You're safe."

She exhales the breath that, really, she's been holding for four years. Then she collapses.

The last thing she remembers is Jacob's tiny voice from the back seat.

"Chet?"

. . .

She wakes to the sound of something dripping. Everything is dark, and she realizes her eyes are closed. She struggles to open them, heavy as they are with fatigue. Her head pounds. Her mouth is like cotton.

Drip. Drip. Drip.

She opens her eyes and stares up at fluorescent lights.

Where am I? she thinks. And then fear consumes her. *Sarah. Jacob.*

But then she remembers the man and the Jeep. The explosion. The crits.

You're safe, he'd said.

Sam. Oh, God, what about Sam?

She tries to move, and realizes there's a needle in her arm attached to an IV bag.

"Mom?"

Rory breathes a sigh of relief. When she turns her head, she sees that Sarah is in a chair next to her. Her daughter looks exhausted, but she's alive.

There is a medical supply cart to Sarah's left, but otherwise the room is bare. The linens are fresh, though, and the linoleum floor reminds her of being at the pediatrician's office with Sarah long ago. What is this place?

"How long have I been out?" Rory asks.

"A day," Sarah answers. "The doctors said it was fatigue, dehydration, and the early stages of hypothermia. They don't know how much longer we would've made it if we hadn't found this place."

"Doctors?" Rory says.

"There's a lot to explain," Sarah says, taking her mom's hand. "But right now, just try to rest. I'm so glad you're awake," she smiles, wiping a tear from her eye.

"Sam?" Rory asks.

"He lost a lot of blood. But he's alive," Sarah pauses. "He hasn't woken up yet."

Rory sighs again, a tear rolling down her cheek. "He will," she whispers.

"I know," she says, putting her hand on Rory's.

It's then that Rory realizes it—her hand feels unbalanced, somehow. She sees it's covered in a bandage. "What…" she begins.

Sarah looks down. "You lost your pinky finger," she says. "It was black with frostbite by the time we got here. They think from holding up Sam for so long. I'm sorry."

Rory almost laughs. A pinky finger is a small price to pay to get her family here alive. "I'll live," she smiles.

Sarah grins back. "Good," her daughter says. "Now, get some rest."

2076

Now

Sam

"You did it," says the voice he's missed every day for almost a year. "You kept him safe."

Becca.

"Are you real?" he asks.

"I'm real to you," she answers.

"I miss you so much," he says.

"I miss you too, baby," she says. "But your part isn't over yet. I'll see you when it is."

"I'm so tired," he says.

"I know, but you have to keep going," Becca answers.

"Why?"

"Because they need you."

"I just need to sleep," he says.

"You can sleep," Becca says gently. "But eventually, you have to go back."

He relaxes. He closes his eyes. Had he even opened them?

The darkness returns.

. . .

He floats in and out of space and time after that. Sometimes seeing Becca, sometimes not. He hears other voices come in and out of his consciousness. Some he knows immediately, but then there is another—one that he knew from another life, maybe. He knows that there is something important he'd set out to do, but doesn't know what it is. Doesn't care what it is, not anymore. Something tells him he can finally rest. But something else tells him he needs to remember—he needs to come back.

But he is tired.

2076

Now

Sarah

Now that her mom is finally awake, she splits her time between her mom's room and Sam's, where Jacob and Chet are constant guests. The doctors monitor Sam closely and have said that he's improving every day. But still, the sight of him lying there—somewhere between reality and the unconscious world—is almost unbearable. The four of them had found something out there on the road together. And she can't give it up. They all need to be okay, together. Sam needs to wake up and see the place they'd worked so hard to reach.

It is so much more than what they'd hoped for.

There are thousands of people here from all over North and South America who'd heard the broadcast and made their way to Canada. Sarah can barely remember ever seeing so many people. Many times she hadn't even dared to hope that this place could really exist.

In her first few days, she learned that Chet, the man who had saved them, knew Sam and Jacob. They'd traveled hundreds of miles together and been separated not long before she'd met them. It is nothing short of a miracle that they'd all made it here. Now, Chet and Jacob spend nearly every moment together. Chet makes sure Jacob gets at least three meals a day, plenty of sleep, and—most importantly—a feeling of real safety. Chet does most of the talking, of course, while Jacob listens, wide-eyed and smiling.

. . .

One afternoon when her mother is resting, Sarah ducks out of her hospital room to join Chet and Jacob for lunch. The old shopping mall's food court has been turned into a mess hall, using the old cooking equipment they'd been able to salvage. There is an entire kitchen staff made up of volunteers. At first, the mess hall was so overwhelming it made her nervous. The sound of all those people talking, laughing, telling stories had nearly made her turn around the first time she tried to go get a meal, but the smells were too intoxicating. Freshly baked bread, roasted vegetables, and even chocolate. It had all been such a distant memory to her. And to Jacob, it may as well have been a different planet. Most days he still has to latch onto her or Chet's hand just to gather up the courage to sit down.

The mess hall is always crowded with people, and today is no exception. As she weaves her way through the crowd, people smile and wave to her, say hello, and introduce themselves.

"It's a little weird for the first couple of weeks," the woman next to her in line for food says. "The socialization can be a lot after years of nothing. You'll get used to it," she smiles.

"Thank you," Sarah says, smiling back. "It's weird, but… in a good way. If that makes sense?"

"It makes perfect sense," the woman says. "My family and I got here about six months ago, and I'm still not always used to it. I still have nightmares, sometimes. About the crits."

Sarah looks at her and nods, "Me too."

"We're not alone in that," the woman says. "It's pretty common. But there's always people to talk to."

"Thanks," Sarah says again, nodding as the woman takes her tray over to join her family.

Sarah fills her lunch tray up with foods she hasn't seen in years—fresh fruits and vegetables. Bread. Pasta. When she's satisfied, she turns and spots Chet and Jacob sitting a few tables away. There is another man sitting with them, someone Sarah has seen around before. He looks to be in his mid-thirties, with bright green eyes that remind her of Jacob.

"Sarah," Chet smiles as she sits down at their table. "This is Gabe. He founded this safe house a few years ago. He's the voice over the broadcast."

She feels like she's meeting a celebrity. "Wow," she says. "It's really you?"

Gabe smiles and extends a hand. "It's nice to meet you," he says. His handshake is firm. "How are you liking the place so far?"

"Beats the road any day," she replies, taking a bite of a strawberry. The flavor explodes in her mouth, and she can't help but sigh.

"Here, here," says Chet, raising his glass of water.

"Your accommodations are okay? Getting enough sleep?" Gabe asks.

"I don't ever remember sleeping this well, honestly," Sarah says. She and her mother have one of the hundreds of make-shift apartments in the safe house. It's small, but it's the best bed she's had in years. "It's a really great thing you made here. I can't believe I'm finally meeting you," she laughs, looking up at Gabe again. She notices, again, how similar his eyes are to

Jacob's. There is a sereness about him that feels kind, if not a little unnatural.

"I've heard your voice about a thousand times on the radio," she says to him. "How did you do all of this?"

"A lot of time and effort," Gabe says. He looks sideways at Chet, then back to Sarah. "You know," he continues, "there are a few things we like to debrief the newcomers on when they arrive."

Chet's eyes dart to him. A warning.

"What things?" Sarah asks.

"Just some things about our plans for the future," says Gabe.

Chet clears his throat. "Things we don't need to burden you with yet," he says, more to Gabe than to her. "Let's give it some time. See how Sam's feeling when he wakes up, eh?"

Sarah's curiosity bubbles. "What are you talking about?" she asks, again, unable to look away from Gabe's bright eyes.

Chet sighs, "I told you to wait," he says, looking at Gabe. "She's just a kid."

But Sarah doesn't feel like a kid anymore. Not after what she went through to get here.

She levels her gaze at Chet. "Tell me," she says.

Chet takes a deep breath and looks up at the ceiling, as if he's deciding something. "Oh, what the hell," he says, and nods to Gabe.

2076

Now

Rory

Two days after Rory, and three days after they arrive, Sam finally wakes up.

He comes slowly back to reality, as if he's being pulled back from some abyss. At first, like she was, he's disoriented. When that passes, he's frightened, and when that passes, he's relieved.

Jacob races into Sam's room after the doctors give them the news, jumping onto the bed to hug him, squeezing his wounded shoulder. Rory sees Sam flinch, but knows he doesn't care. They are here. They are safe. That's all that matters.

We did it.

Chet and Sarah follow into the room after Jacob.

She watches Sam's eyes widen at the sight of Chet. His mouth falls open.

"Oh my God," he says. "How—"

"I'm so happy you made it," Chet says. "I knew you would." The old man's smile is what finally cracks Sam, and he sobs as Chet leans down to embrace him.

As Rory and Sarah leave to give them some privacy, she hears Chet whisper, "She would be so proud of you."

. . .

Over the next few days, Sam and Rory both get strong enough to take a tour of the safe house. Rory takes it at a slow walk while Chet pushes Sam in a wheelchair. Rory's parents had told her once how shopping malls had been all but extinvt until the darkness covered more group. Shipping became too unreliable, so people had to do their shopping locally. This one, Rory could see, must've been under construction before The Collapse. Tarps and scaffolding had been left behind in the cramble and a thick layer of dust covered most of the less-trafficked areas. But the updates Gabe had made were incredible.

There is an entire medical facility—where she and Sam had both just spent the last several days—made up of doctors who'd found their way here over the years. Gabe has spent his time here collecting supplies, and still sends out groups every week to get what they can from the city beyond. There is an enormous garden at one wing with a fully sustainable ecosystem, supplying all these people with the nutrients they so desperately need. A couple of the old stores have been converted into school rooms, with several grades' worth of children and a handful of teachers who'd made the journey north. There is even an old guitar store where someone gives lessons with the instruments that were left behind in pristine condition. But mostly, Rory can't get over how many kids there are. And there's something similar about most of them that she can't quite place.

"So," she asks Chet as they walk. "How do they get the heat and lights working?"

"Couple of fuel runs every few months," Chet says. "And then we cover the windows with old blackout curtains in the lit areas, just in case it would attract the crits."

Rory nods. "That explosion behind us, that night you saved us," she says. "What *was* that?"

"We had it rigged in case of emergency. An entire wall of explosives if the crits ever got too close."

"So, it *did* kill them, then?" Sam chimes in, turning his head from his wheelchair. "I didn't even realize they could be killed."

"Oh yes, they certainly can," Chet says. Rory wants to push for more, but the walk and the information overload are both taking a toll on her.

"I need to sit down," she says.

"There are some couches just up here," Chet answers. "We can take a break."

They stop in an old jewelry store that has been converted into a lounge. There are couches, shelves of books, and there is even a makeshift fire pit in the middle of the room.

A man waits for them there.

"Rory, Sam, this is Gabe," says Chet. "He's the one who started this place a few years back and put out the broadcast."

Rory reaches out a hand. "Wow," she says, noticing how striking the man's eyes are. "It's weird to put a face to the voice on the radio. I can't imagine how much work went into this. Thank you."

"Thank *you* for following the broadcast," Gabe says. "We always love getting new people."

Rory can hear a slight accent in his speech but can't place it.

"So are you from Calgary, then?" Sam asks. "Is that why you decided on this location?"

Gabe doesn't answer, but smiles and looks at Chet. "So you haven't told them?" he asks.

Rory looks around, confused, and sees a knowing glance

pass between everyone. Everyone but her and Sam. They look at one another uneasily.

Chet sighs. "Keep an open mind," he says. "Let's get this over with."

Rory's heart sinks.

"What's going on?" Rory asks, looking over at Sarah.

"It's okay, Mom. Gabe can explain everything," her daughter says, tapping the couch cushion beside her. "Come sit next to me."

. . .

"I know you heard our broadcast about the ships we had left," Gabe starts. He has a soft, gentle way of speaking. Though Rory is still on her guard, she can't help but like him instantly.

Rory looks at Sam. "About that," she says, the disappointment hitting her again. "We were told, by a pretty reputable source, that the ships are pointless. That the crits have already reached Mars."

Gabe and Chet exchange a look.

"I'm sorry," Rory says. "We would've told you sooner, but…"

"It's quite alright," Gabe says. "There are no ships here, anyway. We lied."

"What?" Rory and Sam say at once. She feels her face heat. *It's a trap it's a trap it's a trap.*

"You led us here for nothing?" Sam says.

"I'm sorry," Gabe answers. "It was the only way we knew people would come."

"By lying to them?" Rory looks around, feeling like she might vomit. "What the hell is going on here then?" She starts to reach instinctively toward Sarah. "Why did you bring us here?"

"To fight," Sarah says. They all turned to look at her.

Rory shuts her eyes and lets out a long breath.

"We're leaving," she says evenly, looking at Sam, who nods. "We can't help you." She stands to leave.

"We're *not* leaving," says Sarah.

Rory freezes, turning to look at her daughter. "We. Are. *Leaving*," Rory says firmly.

"Then you'll leave alone," says Sarah. "I'm staying."

Rory stares at her daughter, whose mouth is set in a hard line, eyes unflinching.

"Sarah—" Sam starts.

"No," she interjects. "Will you both just listen? Think about my dad, think about Becca. They died so that we could have a chance. And now we have one."

"What are you talking about?" says Rory.

"Let's just back up for a second," Chet says, putting his hands up in surrender. "Sam, you trust me, right?"

Sam hesitates, but nods after a few seconds.

"I wouldn't be here if it wasn't something worth staying for," Chet says. "Gabe, go on."

Gabe takes a deep breath. "Many of those kids you've seen here," he says, "they're just like Jacob. They can move things without touching them. Hurt the arachs—or crits, as you all call them—even kill them. But…they're just *kids*."

Rory thinks about Jacob, how small and scared he'd looked when they were running towards the safehouse with the crits bearing down on them, being forced to defend them even in his terror. She and Sam would never let him fight them, not now. Maybe not ever.

"There are *others*?" she asks. "How many? I…where did they come from?"

Again, that look passes between everyone except her and Sam. Rory is annoyed that she'd slept for so long. What had she missed?

Gabe lifts his hand, palm open. Just like she'd seen Jacob do before. Behind her, she hears metal dragging across the floor. She turns around to see a chair in front of her, levitating in mid-air.

Before she can speak, the steel chair crumples into a ball like a piece of paper.

Rory leaps out of her chair as Sam shouts, *"What the hell?"*

Rory brings a shaking hand to her mouth and realizes she's moved to stand in front of her daughter. "Whatever this is," she says, "just leave us the fuck alone. We've been through enough."

"Wait, Mom," she feels Sarah take her hand. "Just listen to him, okay?"

She turns to her daughter. "What is going on here?"

"Him and Jacob," Sarah says. "They're from the same place."

Slowly, she turns back to Gabe. Again, she takes in his eyes, realizing that she's seen them a hundred times before. In Jacob.

"You're one of them," she says. It isn't a question.

Gabe nods.

"How?"

"They hit our planet too," Gabe says. "The same exact way they did it here. We'd been destroying our planet for years, same as you. We were worried, of course, about what would happen to us with all the pollution. Where would we go if we destroyed the whole planet? But we never once thought about what that kind of damage would allow *in*. All this time, we thought it was because the atmospheres of our planets are so similar. But if they've reached Mars, maybe there's no method to their destruction."

Rory's cringes.

"It started with the darkness," Gabe continued. "People turned on each other. Crime skyrocketed. And then the arachs—or, crits—came. They wiped out entire cities in a matter of days. And it was then that we knew…we couldn't stay. So, some of the people left made a plan to try and save the next generation."

Rory looks at Jacob, who watches Gabe intently.

"How?" she asks Gabe. "How did you end up here?"

"The U.S. and several other countries have been sending signals into space for decades," Gabe said. "We picked them up on our planet, Salvaris, years ago. Translators spent years deciphering the messages, learning your languages. That's why myself, several of the other stewards, and many of the older children you'll meet can speak with you. We'd been planning to leave Salvaris for about a year, but then—just like here—the darkness started to expand more quickly."

"Hang on," Sam says. "So are you…human?"

Gabe smiles. "We are. And we aren't. Like I said, our planets are very similar, and we suspect many others are as well. Nearly identical atmospheres, similar gravitational pull, and so much more. Turns out our inherent nature is similar, too. Destroying our planets, and all that."

Despite everything, Rory almost smiles. "So, what happened?"

"We took as many children as we could, as well as a few stewards—like myself—and boarded our ships to Earth.

We landed here, but it was a disaster. The darkness had expended so quickly that when the launch came, the arach—crits—descended on us," he pauses, looking at Jacob. The boy is somewhere else. "There was no time. So many died… but many of the stewards stayed back to fight them off while some of us got out. Our ships landed all over Earth, and that's why we sent out the broadcast. Anyone from my home who hears it will know what it means. And we're getting more and more each day. Thousands of us escaped. Millions didn't. We wanted a fresh start…or at least a *chance* for the next generation. But by the time we got here…the crits were already here."

Rory can't imagine it. One final chance at a new life and they'd landed here. It was cruel.

"So what happened when you got here?" Sam asks.

"Some of us landed near Calgary, but some didn't," he turns to Jacob again. "Many of Jacob's shipmates died in the crash landing, including the steward who was with them. His mother."

Chet puts a thick arm around Jacob's shoulders.

"Myself and a few others wandered this area for a while, joining with others from your planet who were already here. When we found this abandoned building, we started to plan."

"But that plan doesn't involve an escape?" Rory whispers.

"No, it doesn't," Gabe answers. "It's clear that the crits are expanding—they're here, as they were on Salvaris, and now you've told me they're on Mars as well. As far as we know, our kind—and some of your weapons on earth—are the only things capable of killing them."

Rory remembered the explosions. "Until the other night, I'd never seen one be killed."

"Neither had I," Chet says. Then he turns to Sam, "but that night, when I drove off in the Jeep, that crit stopped chasing me," he says.

"Why?" Sam asked.

"I saw it limping behind me when I was a few miles away, and then it just stopped. I remembered that psycho had shot it a bunch of times, and I thought—well, I hoped—it was dead. I turned back to check it out, and sure enough, it was."

Rory's jaw drops. She'd always kept her rifle on her as they walked, but it was more of a mental help than she thought it was a physical one. Maybe it would buy them a few seconds, but she'd thought they were unkillable, until Jacob.

"So what's your plan, then?" Rory asks Gabe.

"To stay here, for as long as we need to in order to grow our numbers. To let the children grow up around friends, to learn, to be kids. And then, when they're old enough and if they're willing, to fight."

"Raise them up to die later?" Sam scoffs.

"Or to win," Gabe says. "We have a saying where I'm from: *if you must accept defeat, do it fighting for something you love.* There's nothing I love more than my people, and now, *your* people, too. We could start here, and if we win, we really *could* find the ships that are left. We could help others out there," he looks to the sky.

Rory closes her eyes. "I thought we were coming here for a new beginning," she says.

"You are," Gabe answers. "I will not ask you to fight. That decision, when the time comes, will be entirely yours. But I will ask you to stay, because I know your life here—however long or short it may be—will be better than the one out there."

He stands up, nodding to Chet, who seems to have made

his decision long ago.

"I know you have a lot to discuss," Gabe says. "I hope you will consider staying."

. . .

When Matt died, Rory spent months thinking over and over how much she needed to talk to him, to consult his opinion, to get his thoughts on something. And then she would remember he was dead. This entire thought process would take about one-tenth of a second. *I need to talk to Matt. But Matt is dead.*

That thought hasn't struck her in years. But it does now.

I need to talk to Matt. But Matt is dead.

She looks around at her friends, her family. How could she put them in danger? But maybe the better question is, how could she not give them the best chance they can hope for?

_2076_

Now

Sam

"So, where do we stand?" Sam asks Rory. They've been discussing Gabe's offer for hours.

"Whatever we do, we do it together," Rory says.

It's late. In fact, it's now early. This decision has taken up their entire night.

"I just…" he starts. "I just can't believe after everything, there's no real hope."

"Well," Rory says. "I don't know about that."

He looks at her, eyebrows raised. "What?"

"Jacob was enough to give me hope," she continues. "I mean, knowing how many of them there are, and adults like that? What if Gabe was right? What if we really can beat them?"

"They're kids!"

"They're kids _now_," she says. "It's not like this war is gonna happen tomorrow. And what other choice do we have?"

He knows this, at least, is true.

"We can't go back out on the road, Sam."

He sighs. "I know."

He knows she's right. There is no other choice. This war may not come for years, and when that time comes, he can only hope that Jacob will be old enough to make his own decision about fighting.

At 5 a.m., they reach their decision. They'll stay. And when the time comes, they'll fight.

. . .

Since it's already morning, they head down to the mess hall in search of the strongest coffee available after a night of no sleep. Sam's head is pounding. He's decided to forgo the wheelchair today, but he's still recovering and wants nothing more than to rest. But he knows it's futile. He doesn't realize yet how long it will take his body to recover from being in a constant state of fight or flight—how long it will take for his nervous system to realize that he is, after so many years, finally safe.

Despite seeing much of the safe house yesterday, Sam is still blown away by what Gabe has done with the place. It's almost unnerving to see so much light after spending the last two and a half years in total darkness. His eyes are still trying to adjust, having become so sensitive on the road. It's strange to see this intersection of the old world and the new. There are stores in this once-mall that he used to be so familiar with, but has forgotten about over time. The old signs remind him that there were people here once doing their Christmas shopping. People came here to get their ears pierced, to eat lunch, to try on a new outfit for a date. Who could've predicted what would become of this place?

He still fears that this is all a dream he'll soon wake up from only to be thrust back into the terrors of the outside world. He has to keep reminding himself that this is, in fact, real.

In the mess hall, only a few other very early risers have the same idea about breakfast. Among the early birds are Chet and Gabe. They each have a steaming mug of coffee set in front of them and they appear to be in the middle of a deep conversation. When Sam and Rory approach, the two cut their chat short, but not before Sam hears a few words.

"They're good people," Chet whispers. "They deserve to know—"

"Morning," Gabe says loudly, cutting Chet off.

Sam looks between them—Chet looking uncomfortable, Gabe with an easy smile. "Morning," Sam says. "We, uh, discussed your offer."

Gabe perks up. "I didn't mean for you to lose sleep over it," he says, surveying them. "My apologies. You could have, of course, taken as much time as you needed."

"We're staying," Rory says flatly. Then she looks at Sam and reaches out, squeezing his good shoulder. "And we'll fight."

Chet and Gabe both smile, but Sam can see the sadness behind their eyes. This means that in some way, they'll get a life. But just how long would that life be?

"Thank you," Gabe says. "I know that couldn't have been an easy decision."

"I'm glad you're staying," Chet says with a smile, standing up to clap Sam on the shoulder. "I was afraid it would get boring around here again."

Sam laughs and eyes his friend for a long moment, realizing how tired the old man looks. Chet has aged in the time they've been apart. His wrinkles are more pronounced, his face slightly hollower. His hair leans toward completely white. But the kindness has never left those blue eyes, no matter what he'd seen on his journey to get here.

"What were you talking about just now?" Sam asks him. "You said 'they deserve to know.' What do we deserve to know?"

Chet clicks his tongue and looks at Gabe pointedly. "Well?" he says.

Gabe clears his throat. "If you're up for it," he says. "There's...one more thing I think you're ready to see, now that you've decided to stay."

"Just when I was starting to like you," Sam sighs, squinting at Gabe.

Gabe smiles. "If you'd like to grab some coffee," he says, "then you can follow me."

2078

Now

Jacob

Finally, after two years, he's home. Or at least, as close to home as he can get.

His alarm blares across the room, letting him know it's 6 a.m. Even though it's been two years, he never altered from their schedule out on the road. Here, structure is everything.

He rubs his eyes and yawns before stepping out of bed to shut off the alarm. He can smell the coffee Sam and Chet are already making in the kitchen of their apartment. No matter how many times he's asked, Sam has told him he's not allowed to drink coffee regularly until he's fifteen. Something about stunting his growth, which Jacob is skeptical of, given that he's not even really human.

His friend Cade groans and throws a hand over his eyes across the room. When Jacob got here a few years ago, he couldn't believe some of the other boys he'd been with on his ship from Salvaris had made it. Reuniting with them was the closest to home Jacob had ever felt. Now, with so many new arrivals over the last few years, a lot of them are bunking together. He, Cade, Sam, and Chet are all in one small apartment, but that doesn't bother any of them. They've all lost too much to care about being in close quarters.

"Time to wake up, sunshine!" Jacob says, throwing a pillow at Cade's head. Jacob's English has improved tenfold in the last two years. To the untrained ear, he sounds like a native.

"Uuurrrgghh," Cade answers.

Jacob laughs as he pulls on his other sock, getting dressed for training before school.

. . .

"Bacon?" Chet asks when Jacob sits down at the table.

"Yes please," Jacob answers.

Chet shovels a pile onto his plate, Jacob's mouth already watering.

"How's work?" Jacob asks.

"Oh, let's see," Chet says. "Finished up lunar field #1, should be starting construction on the next greenhouse when Gabe's group gets back with supplies this week, and we got the water purifier back up and running, thankfully."

Chet works as the self-proclaimed handyman of the safehouse, managing all the sustainable energy projects to keep the place running and habitable, and hopefully to start fixing what the humans had broken long ago.

"Light work," Sam jokes as he takes his seat.

"Just another day in paradise," Chet grins.

"What's on the docket at training this morning?" Sam asks, looking at Jacob.

"Forcefields," Jacob says. "A defensive measure to protect each other from attacks."

"You'll have to show me when you get home," Sam says.

"*After* your schoolwork."

"How's your training going?" Cade asks Sam from the living room as he makes his way over to the table. "I heard Sarah is getting really good."

Chet smiles. "*Getting* good? Where have you been for the last few years?"

It's true, Sarah has excelled to become one of the top performers at hand-to-hand combat in her training class. A lot of pent-up rage, Jacob thinks.

"She's still the best," Sam says. "Although that new girl, Sydney? She's giving her a run for her money."

"Really?" Cade asks, finally joining them. The kid loves a good piece of gossip.

"Yeah, they're going to be trouble, I think," Sam says, shaking his head.

Jacob smiles. He's heard about Sydney, alright. Sarah has become his closest confidant over the last few years. The older sister he never had.

All four of them head out at the same time. Sam heads to the gym for training with Sarah's class, he and Cade to the old library, which is now used as the Salvaris training room, and Chet to whichever job is the most urgent that week.

As Jacob and Cade break away, they pass by Paul's memorial, stopping to read the plaque that Gabe created after they told everyone what Paul had done for them. The inscription was short, but always brought tears to Jacob's eyes when he saw it.

For Paul, who gave his life for his friends.
We will never forget you.

Paul, like Becca and his parents, gave his life to keep Jacob alive. He remembers it every time he and his friends talk about Paul. Every time Sam's eyes mist over when he shares a memory about Becca. Every time he misses his parents so much he can barely stand. But now he understands that family isn't always blood. Because whenever he looks at Rory, Sarah, Chet, Cade, and Sam, he knows he *does* still have a family. And that maybe, somewhere, his parents are happy about that.

2081

Now

Sarah

Finally, in all the chaos of the morning, she has a moment alone. She stands in the bridal suite in a white dress that her mother gifted her after finding it in an old department store. She stares at herself, not believing this moment is real. Just five years ago, she didn't think she'd make it here at all. And now, it's the morning of her wedding.

She hears her mother open the door quietly and come in, appearing next to her in a few strides. She's wearing a floor-length, eggplant satin dress. Her hair has grown out since they've been here, now reaching well past her shoulders. Her scar has faded over the years and she looks stunning as she places a gentle hand on Sarah's shoulder.

"You look beautiful," her mother says.

Sarah smiles. "So do you, Mom," she pauses, gathering herself. "Is this real?"

Her mother laughs. "It's real," she says. "I can't believe you're getting married at twenty."

Sarah laughs. "It feels normal to me."

"I was young when I got married, too," her mom says. "Why wait?"

It's a common saying around the safe house now, after everything everyone has been through. *Why wait?*

She doesn't feel twenty. She feels like an old woman. She looks at her arms, lean with muscle and dotted with bruises from training. Her hair, usually in a braid, flows down her back in soft curls from the rollers her mother had done for her last night. Her eyes, that had never quite adjusted to the light, are lined with mascara. She thinks about the rest of her life with Sydney, however short it may be.

"Ready?" her mom whispers.

"Ready," she says.

They link arms and head for the door, through the mess hall, and over to the old movie theater, which is used for these ceremonies now. She knows that on either side of the aisle, she'll see people she's grown to love. New friends, old friends, and her family—Sam, Chet, and Jacob, who will be waiting in the front row.

Her mom squeezes her arm, and they step out into the aisle.

Their last walk north together.

2091

Now

Rory

The years have passed quickly, as if life were taunting them—now that they'd finally reached a safe, happy place, time would be taken from them too fast. It's remarkable how many people have shown up in the last fifteen years. They have tens of thousands now. And while Chet has gotten older, he hasn't lost much steam. Keeping the lights on, the greenhouse plants growing, and the water purified has been an astronomical task for this many people. But he has a team of hundreds helping him now. Rory hopes it will make a difference.

"Ready to get breakfast, Rory?" Sydney calls from her and Sarah's room.

As much as she would've loved for Sarah and Sydney to have their own place, there simply isn't enough room for that luxury. Sydney's parents never made it to the safe house, and she's never once complained about their living situation. Rory thinks that some part of her likes having a pseudo mom in the apartment.

"Yep, ready when you are" Rory answers, ignoring the phantom itch in her pinky finger. Fifteen years, and it's never gone away.

The safe house has gotten so overcrowded, the population has to eat at the mess hall in shifts. They like to have breakfast there on weekends, when their shift is the earliest, since none of them could ever stop waking up at 6 o'clock anyway.

. . .

They find Sam, Chet, Jacob, and Cade at their usual table. Sarah and Sydney run over to join the boys. It's been years, but Rory still can't believe how much they've all grown. Jacob is a grown man now who, in the right company—usually Sarah—doesn't shut up. But Rory still remembers that quiet little boy who saved their lives more than once.

She, Chet, and Sam share a knowing look. They have agreed that today is the day, since Gabe let them know that the news will be made public this week, and voting the next.

Instinctively, Sam pulls out the chair next to him so that she can sit. "Morning," he says, sliding her a cup of coffee, just the way she likes it. She thinks of the glasses of wine she poured Matt, all those years ago. Another life.

"You know me too well," she smiles. "Thank you."

Over the years, her friendship with Sam has only grown stronger. She knows that Sarah and Jacob used to wonder if it would ever turn into something more, but she and Sam always knew it wouldn't. There are some things even time can't heal. But in their own way, they've both helped each other come back from the darkness.

Rory looks around at the family she's found and wonders how much longer they'll have like this. How soon will they finally be forced into battle? It's difficult to know. But on the outside, things are nearing a breaking point. They can hear the crits every night now. Their cameras at the perimeter pick up more and more movement each day—it's a complete mystery how any newcomers are still reaching the safe house. But Rory knows, deep down, they can't hold out here much longer.

"Alright," Rory says when she notices everyone finishing their breakfast. "There's something Chet, Sam, and I need to tell you three."

"You're all in a relationship together?" Sydney chimes in. "I knew it."

Sarah swats her wife while the others burst out laughing. Chet nearly swallows his fork.

"Not yet," Rory says, smiling. "Come on, everybody. Follow me."

. . .

She leads them the same way Chet and Gabe had led her and Sam fifteen years ago. To an old bookstore, which now serves as the library, and through a door with a faded "employees only" sign above it. Rory smiles to herself walking under that sign, still feeling like she's doing something she shouldn't be.

"Is this the part where you kill us?" Cade asks, as Rory leads them down the dark hallway behind the door.

"Oh come on," Chet answers, clicking on a flashlight, "even *we're* not that unoriginal."

"I didn't even realize there were parts of the safe house that weren't lit anymore," Sarah says.

"This is the only secret left," Chet says. "And it won't be a secret much longer."

Rory looks back and sees the kids—she'll always think of them as kids—exchange a look.

She leads them to an elevator, which takes them down several stories below the earth. When the doors open, there is another hallway and a steel door protected by a keypad, where Rory punches in the code.

"Are you *sure* you're not going to kill us?" Cade says again, this time with a touch of wariness in his voice.

"We're almost there," Rory says.

Rory throws the door open and they emerge into a circular room lit with sconce lights. Each one points downward to spotlight a small, enclosed bed, large enough for one person. The room is filled with them.

"Well, this is creepy," Sarah says. "What is all this?"

"This room used to act as security for the mall," Chet says. "But now, it has…a different purpose," he waves his hand at the beds.

"What are those?" Sydney says.

Rory takes a deep breath. "These are hibernation capsules," she says, standing over one of the beds, "There were, apparently, several on each ship leaving Salvaris, for emergency use only. Most were destroyed in the crash landings. But Gabe and his crew were able to save these ones."

"I think I remember these," Jacob says, running a hand over the smooth glass cover of one of the capsules. Next to him, brow furrowed, Cade is nodding. "A hibernation capsule," Jacob goes on. "You don't mean…" he trails off.

"That's exactly what I mean," Rory answers.

"What are you guys talking about?" Sarah asks. "What is a hibernation capsule?"

"It's a device that allows the person inside to be, essentially, frozen as they are now," Sam says. "And to sleep until they're woken up, at some point in the future. You could sleep for a hundred years, a thousand…as many as you want. The hibernation system stops you from aging during that time. They tested them on Salvaris, and there seemed to be no cognitive damage, either. But…we can't really be sure." He looks skeptical.

The room is silent for a moment.

"So why are you showing this to us?" Sydney asks.

"Because before the battle, we're going to vote on who gets a spot in each capsule," Chet says. "We need to be realistic about this coming war," he goes on, sighing heavily. "It's likely going to kill most of us, and who knows how many people will be left, if any are left at all? The ones in the capsules would, really, be our best chance at a new life in the future. They would at least get to see if we succeed here. Or if we fail."

The room is silent, the weight of those words settling over them all.

Sarah looks stunned. "But how can you know that they'll even wake up? If the crits win, or if the earth even survives?"

"We can't," Rory replies. "We can't know if they'll wake up, or what kind of world they'll wake up to, or if there will *be* a world to wake up in at all. Whoever decides to enter their name in the vote will understand the risks and have to make their own decision."

"So...why are you telling *us*?" Sydney asks again.

"Because I asked Gabe to tell them, a long time ago," Chet says, gesturing to Rory and Sam. "I'd done several favors for Gabe in my time at the safe house. I wanted Sam and Rory to know that, no matter what happens, there's still a chance for a future," he pauses there, looking at Sarah, Sydney, Jacob, and Cade for a moment. "A future for you four, if you enter the vote," he finishes.

"*You* wouldn't enter the vote?" Sarah asks, looking at Rory.

"It wouldn't be fair," Rory answers. "I'm almost fifty years old. We should let the future be in the hands of young people."

"And if I don't want to enter?" Sarah says, flustered. "I mean, this is insane."

Rory smiles. "Then I'd support you, whatever you decide. But our chances here…they're slim. The only thing I've ever wanted is what's best for you. And I know this is it."

"Jesus," Cade says under his breath. "I need a minute."

"We know it's a lot," Sam responds.

"You lied to us this whole time," Sarah says. "You kept this from us."

Sydney puts a hand on Sarah's shoulder.

"I'm sorry," Rory answers. "We didn't want you to be afraid or have anything else heavy on your minds. We just wanted you to be kids, and grow up, and find love," she looks at Sydney. "But I'm begging you all, please enter the vote. This is the best chance you have. Even if we win the war, who knows what the other side of it would look like?"

"Sarah," Jacob says. "She's right."

"What?" Sarah says.

"I don't like this any more than you do," Jacob continues. "But she's right. This is the best hope for humanity. It's people taking the biggest risk of their lives, but otherwise…the entire human race could be wiped out."

"You can't be serious," Sarah says.

"I *am* serious," Jacob replies. "Do you know how much I wish we'd done this on Salvaris, so that maybe more people would have had a chance?"

"So you'd want to just climb into this thing," Sarah says, eyes boring into Jacob, "with no clue about where or when you'll wake up, or even *if* you'll wake up?"

"No," Jacob sighs. "I don't. I'll be a much greater asset to the war than you. No offense," he adds, then looks at Sarah and Sydney. "But both of you need to enter the vote."

FALL 2095

Rory

I'VE WRITTEN AS MUCH OF OUR STORY AS I CAN, as best as I can remember it, so that when you wake up, you can start to remember it, too. I'm hopeful that getting a letter from me will help, no matter how many centuries have passed. But really, I have no idea. It is, like this entire decision, just my best guess. We programmed the pods to wake you up exactly five hundred years from now, but we provided instructions for others to wake you up before then, if they find you.

It's been 23 years since The Collapse. Nineteen since we arrived at the safe house in Calgary. Three since I watched you and Sydney go into hibernation and the war began. Six months since it ended.

At perhaps the most extensive loss of life Earth has ever seen, we won.

The two-and-a-half-year conflict felt like nothing but radiation and bloodshed. It only reinforced how happy I was that you weren't here to witness it. We kept detailed logs of everything. Of how the crits almost overtook us in several battles, of cities lost and won, of more people found out there—still alive—ready and eager to help us fight.

We lost Sam. Chet and I planted his ashes in one of the greenhouses he's restoring so that one day, maybe when you wake up, a part of him will still be here. I think he would've liked that.

Gabe, Cade, and Jacob were incredible. You would've been so proud. They've already started constructing a few ships to take them and a small army back to Salvaris, then onto Mars, where they'll keep fighting.

So for now, it's just me and Chet. He's about eighty now and still fit as ever. Most days, we read and work on re-building the sustainable energy systems that were destroyed in the war. Just going through the motions with the other survivors. Mainly, we talk about you, Sydney, Jacob, and Sam. We miss you so much.

At this point, you're probably wondering why I haven't woken you up. The battle is over, the danger from the crits is finally done. So why leave you in the capsule? Trust me when I say it's been the hardest decision I've ever had to make. But it's also the most important one.

The weapons we needed to fight off the crits caused complete and utter destruction to what was left of the Earth. They toxified the atmosphere, ruining most of what was left of any salvageable land and livestock, and making life here now more uncertain than ever. Even with Chet and what remains of his team back at work, who knows how long it will take to restore what's been destroyed? Who knows if we even can? He told me the other day he could've sworn it was getting brighter out there, but I haven't seen any difference. The darkness lingers on. And as your mother, it's my job to take care of you—despite the hopefulness of an old man. It's the only job I've ever known. That's why I've chosen to let you sleep.

Please forgive me.

Know that I visit you every day, but in the end, I know the only future you can possibly have is in another time. Another century. Where things, I hope, are better.

I hope you wake up to a brighter world. I hope you and Sydney get everything you've always wanted. I hope I made the right decision and that the future—no matter what it holds—looks better than it does here now.

I will always love you.

Mom

2445

EPILOGUE

Sarah

"Holy shit," someone says. "It worked. She's waking up!"

At first everything is darkness, as if she is in a dream—or a nightmare. Is she back on the road? How?

Her body stirs, and a great heaviness overcomes her. Her limbs are concrete, her lungs full of glue. She's never felt this tired in her entire life.

What is this?

She gasps for air, the first breath her lungs have drawn on their own in almost 500 years, though she isn't aware enough yet to know that. She isn't aware enough to know anything, except for her body's instinct to survive. She takes another breath. And another. It feels incredible. Had she been drowning?

Her consciousness comes back slowly. She starts to remember, reaching for the memories as if from some great depth. First, she can only remember the darkness. The stars. The cold. The endless walking.

Then she remembers the people. Her mother, Sam, Jacob...but they're all gone. She knows it, even if she can't remember why. Even if she can barely remember anything else.

She hears whispers around her, as if a small crowd has gathered to watch her wake. *Wake up,* she tells herself. *It's time.*

Her eyelids are so heavy from disuse. She fights to lift them open. First one, then the other.

The first thing she sees in this new century is sunlight.

Acknowledgements

THIS BOOK wouldn't have been possible without my amazing publisher, editor, and general wearer of all hats, Hannah Gordon at Gordon Publishing Collective. In fact, it wouldn't even be a book without you. It would still be a novella. Thank you for pushing me and for knowing how much more was left to uncover. You are amazing.

I'd like to give an enormous thank you to my brother, Dan. You have always been my first and most honest reader, whether I wanted to hear your feedback or not. Thank you for believing in this story and convincing me to try and get it published.

To my amazing beta readers Dan, Holly, Emily, and Nate, I can never thank you enough. Your notes were invaluable. Thank you for your honesty, expertise, and grace.

What is a book without a cover? Marissa, you are exceptional. Thank you, from the bottom of my heart, for seeing me, for seeing my work, and for bringing it to life.

Mom and Dad, thank you for always encouraging me to to pursue my passion of writing, but to get a day job first. You were right. The tax man comes for us all!

Finally, to my amazing life partner, dog co-parent, and best friend. Mike, I couldn't have done any of this without your support. Thank you for being my rock. Forever and ever, babe.

About the Author

EMILY MULCAHEY grew up in Henniker, New Hampshire, and pursued her passion for storytelling at St. Bonaventure University, where she earned a degree in sociology with a minor in journalism & mass communication. After graduation, she moved to Madrid, Spain, to teach English and explore Europe—an adventure that would, inevitably, give her a lot to write about. Now an accomplished writer at an advertising agency, Emily continues to weave stories that capture both heart and imagination. When she's not at her desk, you'll find her traveling, reading, or enjoying time with loved ones. *Take Care of Our Daughter* is her debut novel.

Discover more about Emily's writing journey on her personal blog at emilymulcahey.wordpress.com.

About the Publisher

Ink is black, sticky, and stubborn. When spilled, it stains—leaving behind a mark that lingers, a reminder of the moment it escaped its container. Whether we knocked it over ourselves or someone else did, we all find ourselves sitting in spilt ink at some point.

But it's not the ink itself that defines us—it's what we do with it. At Spilt Ink Press, we embrace the chaos and mess of life's spills, transforming them into works that illuminate the human condition. We are a genre-crossing imprint devoted to literary works, magical realism, science fiction, historical narratives, poetry, and collections of short stories and novellas—stories that dive deep into the complexity and resilience of the human spirit.

For us, spilt ink is more than a metaphor; it's a call to action. It's the reminder that even in the mess, there's magic waiting to be discovered. We champion bold, imaginative voices that find beauty in the chaos and authenticity in the scars. Our mission is to bring these stories to light, creating a space for works that challenge, inspire, and connect.

Life's stains are inevitable, but they don't have to be wasted. Let's craft stories that linger, art that endures, and wonders that rise from the spills. At Spilt Ink Press, we don't just clean up the mess—we create from it.